# THE SHIPWRIGHT OF TRANSMARINIA

### LAIR
#### ◄ •6• ►

I0694650

TP

TRANSMARINIA PRESS

ISBN for ebook: 978-1-966623-02-1
ISBN for paperback: 978-1-96623-03-8

For readers 18+. Contains descriptions of sex and violence.

Cover design by Trif Book Design.

Transmarinia Press
2709 N Hayden Island Dr
STE 330550
Portland, OR 97217

*It wasn't abandonment
if they weren't meant for you*

# ONE

When I peer through the periscope of the *Lady Revenge*, I can't deny it.

It all feels wrong.

It shouldn't. What I see in those bleary crosshairs is a paradise of jagged reefs, brilliant tropical waters sparkling with sunlight. A flawless postcard vacation destination.

Flawless, that is, except for the foreboding sight of Commodore Volok's yacht.

My throat works in a swallow. "She's dropped anchor."

Adrian Voper shifts behind me, as restless as a caged animal. "Dropped anchor?"

I nod, my eyes suctioned to the rubber eyeguards of the periscope. "Like she's waiting."

Adrian runs a hand through the curly bramble of his hair, his handsome face taut. We've been following the *Keep* for what feels like ages now, and though Adrian has been in phone contact with Arie, providing support, the stress has left him completely frazzled.

He starts pacing the bridge. "I don't like it. Aurora should have been presented to the Commodore by now."

He halts to check the face of his dazzlingly expensive wristwatch and scowls, lets his hand hang at his side again. He draws in a shaky breath. "Do you—do you think she—"

He doesn't finish the sentence; he doesn't need to. I know what he's thinking.

*Did she fail?*

Yes, the plan has been working. To get close enough to the Commodore to assassinate him, she got herself hired as a stewardess aboard his boat. She used his blood son to get chosen as his bride. Everything has worked out perfectly.

But now, on the day she's to be brought before the Commodore, his yacht has dropped anchor amongst one of Sardinia's enchanting archipelagoes. And that dreamy tropical water? Shallow for miles, which means we'll have to surface our submarine yacht if we want to get closer.

It feels calculated. It feels like a trap.

It feels like the Commodore knows.

I straighten to level a look at Adrian. "Arie is the most resourceful woman I have ever met. And the most stubborn. If anyone is capable of pulling this off, it's her." Something in Adrian relaxes a little, his face shining with helpless gratitude, and I hate myself for adding, "But. It has been a long time."

Adrian's face slackens, all the tentative hope in it vanishing. He begins to pace again, fists clenched, the muscles in his shoulders ridged up in worry and agitation.

At last, he stops. "We have to get closer. If she needs to escape, we need to be on hand." His eyes fix on me. "Do you see anything?"

I duck to check the periscope again, shake my head. "Nothing that I can—"

"Let me see."

I back away to give Adrian a turn at the periscope, waiting a moment before I say my piece. I know he won't like it at all.

"Herr Voper," I warn in a gentle but firm tone. "We're too close. If we're spotted, it doesn't just give us away. It could give Arie away, too—"

Adrian doesn't let go of the handles of the periscope when he pulls his pale face away to look at me. His expression is as cold and implacable as marble. "And if we lose them and Aurora needs me? What then?"

The bridge falls silent. The female crew from Transmarinia turn to me, waiting for my response.

I can't tell them what I'm thinking. I can't tell them of the almost suffocating hatred I've harbored toward the Commodore for centuries. I can't tell them that I don't want to do anything that might jeopardize his demise.

But looking at Adrian now, I also can't help but think of my husband Reinhard. And the things I would do to get him back.

"Please," Adrian whispers, the words raw as chipped stone. "I don't know if I can bear this world without her."

And, apparently, how I'd feel if I heard him say such things to get me back.

I sweep the bridge with my gaze. "Rig for surfacing. Bring us within half a mile of the *Keep*."

The crew nod and scurry to carry out my command. Adrian, satisfied, inclines his head and fits his eyes to the rubber eyeguards of the periscope once more. Watching him, I can't help but wonder if I've doomed his love and my chance at vengeance.

The engines of the *Lady Revenge* hum to life and there's a faint juddering as we rise up toward the glare of day. Maybe everything will be all right. The Commodore doesn't know I built this craft. And I've designed its top half to look like a superyacht when above water, anyway. He has no reason to suspect anything.

Maybe I'm being too cynical, as always.

The immense glass pane of the bridge's viewing gallery lights up with the sun, water dripping down it in a bubbling cascade, and then I don't need a periscope to see the Commodore's yacht.

She's enormous. All gleaming black with three carbon-fibre masts raking the sky, as ominous as a hearse. I remember making her back in Transmarinia, though of course I didn't know who I was making it for, then. Volok has always shrouded himself in secrecy.

The sight of her sends a pang of dread through me.

The hiss of the venting ballast dies away, and then we're cruising slowly toward her. I wait for any movement on that boat, any sign of us being spotted. But there's nothing. She's as deserted as a ghost-ship.

Then Adrian's phone starts ringing.

He darts a look at me, his face tight and difficult to interpret. I know how much pain he's been in lately. Aurora had to do things to be selected as a bride. Letting herself be tasted by the Commodore's blood son had thrown him into a wrenching anguish, and I had never seen him so wounded. I had never seen him in love.

And so the phone has rung and rung by the time he answers it.

"Aurora?" The answer he gets wipes the bitter anger from his face. "Are you okay? How'd it go?" Another look my way. Then his voice drops, becomes as tight as his shoulders as he points a finger at an invisible Aurora. "Baby, whatever they're trying to make you do, don't you fucking do it. Do you understand?"

My stomach drops. It happened. She's been found out. Everything has gone wrong.

"Don't you fucking do it, do you hear me?" Adrian snaps, his voice rising. "I will not let him do that to you—"

There's a gasping on the other end of the line, the sound of Aurora crying. And then Adrian is telling her that he loves her, he will always love her. It raises the goose bumps along my arms.

He is saying goodbye.

I dart to the periscope, rotate the handles to sweep the horizon and find the *Keep*. And when I do, white smoke mushrooms up from her foredeck and I catch the glint of missile shells rushing out of a hidden silo.

So. The Commodore made some upgrades without me.

I whirl to face my crew. "Abandon ship. All of you. Now!"

Horror fills their eyes. Dawning comprehension. There's a rush of panicked bodies, crew members undogging doors and rushing out into the day, screaming as the sun smokes their skin. One of them grabs at me. "Ilsa!" she shrieks.

But I throw a look behind me.

Adrian is still on the phone, rooted to the spot as he gazes out of the viewing gallery toward his love.

We have only moments—seconds—before we're annihilated.

I make my decision.

"Adrian!" I dart back and grab him, haul him toward the door. He does not react. He still has the phone to his ear, is still speaking into it.

"I'll always be with you," he promises. "My Northern Light."

We're stumbling out onto the deck and the burning eye of the sun when I see it. The blur of ballistic missiles traveling four times the speed of sound that no mortal could see, raining down on us. There's no time. No escape. Death is here.

I think of Reinhard, and do the only thing I can.

The impact is like the obliteration of all sound, the winking out of the world in a blinding white flash. It breaks the *Lady Revenge*'s back as if it were punched by a god. She buckles, metal screaming, the shockwave turning the whole sea around her white. A wall of ferocious orange flame roars at us, but I'm already moving. I wrench the steel door clean off the observation tower of the *Lady Revenge* in a squealing of hinges and whirl so I'm standing between Adrian and the explosion, the door held like a shield between us. Adrian's eyes—inches from mine behind a slot of glass in the door—widen in shock at the recognition of what I'm doing for him.

"Go get her," I whisper.

Then the explosion hits us.

It lifts us off our feet and blasts us feet fifty through the air as if we had been hit by a rocket launcher at point-blank range. The pain is indescribable. In an instant all my pale blond hair is incinerated off my blistered scalp. My business suit is blowtorched off my back in a fluttering of scorched rags. Every inch of my skin is charred and bubbled to reveal the raw redness beneath. My very brain feels on fire.

The explosion bounces Adrian and the cooked door away from me. The impact of my bare, barbecued skin on the water should be agony, but I welcome it. The coldness is like a balm. I'm plunged under and for a moment my body catches in place, suspended in a whirling bed of bubbles, and I hear Adrian's voice, very far away, shouting my name.

He's alive. I did it. It was worth it.

Someone else can live for love.

Then my body sinks down, down, down into the gloom.

# TWO

I come to rest in a bower of brightly colored coral, leaving a trail of ash and scraps of blackened flesh hanging in the water above me. All around, the bodies of my crew float to their graves, burnt to husks of charcoal. Among them, like some titan out of myth, the wreckage of the *Lady Revenge*. She sinks in a burning bubble of fire through dreamy fathoms, settles with a gentle boom and rumble on the seabed, kicking up clouds of silt. But this is on the furthest bounds of my awareness; consciousness escapes me. My body is ravaged: my face is crisped and blackened into a charred mask, one half of my ribcage eaten away to show the strings of muscle and gristle clinging to tines of bone. I cannot see anymore: my eyeballs have been seared white, their lashes burnt off. I am in a hot, suffocating darkness. I am ready for sleep.

I let myself dream.

*I see Reinhard . . . I see his sideburns, his curly black hair that brushes the collar of his greatcoat, his eyes like the blue heart of a fire . . . The year is 1755, and he is the most handsome man I have ever seen. He is tall, strong, kind, deep-voiced and well-spoken. He asks after my interests. He wants to know me in ways no man before him has. I melt under his attention . . . Soon, we are taking long walks along the waterfront of Wismar. The high houses around us, the sawing of carpenters, the inlet of the Baltic Sea a dazzle of light green water . . . He is a ship builder. His work is known all throughout Germany. He says he will teach me, if I wish. Of course, I agree. I am madly in love with him . . .*

Around me, in their watery graves, the husks of my crewmates begin to cave in on themselves, time and the gently sucking tides of the Mediterranean pulling their ashes apart. Before long, they have dissipated entirely.

But I am not alone. There is the *Lady Revenge*, rust beginning to mantle her hull. And fish dart by, striped in shimmering colors. They nose up to me and nibble at my body.

My life hangs by a thread. I should not be alive. I should not have survived this.

But I have. I am. I have always been a survivor.

I dream.

*We make love for the first time in his shop, propped up against the lapstraked hull of an upturned ship . . . A hesitancy, stifled laughter, before the waves of pleasure that turn me into someone I do not know—someone who bites, and pleads, and makes ferocious sounds—and who clings to him afterward, my fingers curled in his shirt, sawdust in my hair . . . He promises me a life together. He says he wants a wife who will work alongside him. I can think of nothing I want more . . .*

More fish drift by to investigate. Some are put off by me, the strange properties of my deathless flesh, and others nibble tentatively and dart away.

Then a moray eel scatters them as it approaches, an undulating black ribbon with a wicked seam of jaws.

It wants more than a bite.

*Our reputation spreads across Germany . . . I have taken to his work. Its honest harshness, the building of things adapted to survive where they should not be, suits the forthright and fearless nature I think myself in possession of (this is before I would be aware of my own capacity for survival) . . . In time, my aptitude surpasses even that of my husband's. It attracts the attention of those you wish to never meet . . . One night, there's a knock on the door of our shop. It is the Commodore. Clothed in a mariner's frock coat, his pale fingers like icicles, his head as bald as the moon. I cannot understand his slithering tongue, but there is a translator with him. A butler in tails, his face painted a hideous white, a dot of red on both cheeks. He says they represent a club of esteemed men. They wish to change their way of life and take to the sea. They desire me to build them yachts, each designed to represent the nature of its owner. They would pay well . . .*

*I refuse. The sight of them makes my blood run cold. I know, deep in my bones, that to do as they ask would be to damn myself . . .*

*But they damn me anyway . . .*

The moray eel circles me in a seductive death dance, testing to see if I'm easy prey. Then it slows as it flows up to face me.

It's made its decision.

*There is another man waiting behind the Commodore and his translator. He steps forward now. He smiles at me, and the smile is sharp. It makes the hairs on the back of my neck stand on end . . .*

*Behind him, darkness flows. Clicking, squeaking, screeching. It's a living carpet of rats. Hundreds of them. Noses twitching, black eyes glittering, flowing like a tide with their little claws scrabbling in the sawdust, some of them missing hair in patches, reeking like a plague . . .*

*My whole body horripilates in revulsion . . .*

*And the man is before me now, the rats flowing around him like a cape . . . He grabs me by the hair and sinks two long foreteeth into my neck . . .*

*Reinhard screams . . . He is struck unconscious to the floor . . . I am lying in the blood-soaked sawdust of the shop now, a pool of red spreading around me, the rats skittering and squirming over me in a seething mass, their sharp nails scratching my skin, their hairless tails cold against my flesh, their overpowering rankness stuffing down the scream that wants to get out . . .*

*I know a great evil has been committed against me. I know, in a strange and profound way, that I have been changed . . .*

*When I look up, the Commodore looms above me . . . He bends down and offers a slender hand . . . Come, he tells me. We will take you to your new home . . .*

*My new home, as it turns out, is an island. They call it Transmarinia . . .*

The moray eel ribbons its way up to my face. Its long crack of jaws ungapes, revealing rows of vicious needle-like teeth.

*The rage begins to form in my heart like a sickness. It's not long before I escape the island in a boat I have built and track down my maker, intent on destroying him and freeing myself of this curse . . . But I am stopped before I can get to him . . . The Commodore pinches my face with a hand, forces me to look. For my maker is coming, attended by his plague of rats. He is trotting out my Reinhard . . . He makes him kneel, grabs that curly hair I so love and tilts his head back to bare his neck . . .*

*The Commodore is hissing in my ear. His translator does his work . . .*

*If I do not do as they ask, he says, they will kill my Reinhard. They will kill my love. And they will keep him around for eternity to make sure I stay obedient . . .*

*And as the high-pitched screeches of vermin fill my ears, my maker sinks his fangs into my love's neck . . .*

The moray eel lunges for my face, fangs ready to hook into my skin . . .

*When I'm dragged back to that accursed island, I know: I will never get away. But through the long years, that rage in me builds, as incandescent as a sun . . . I think of killing myself . . . I think of ending this pain . . . And yet, I brood on vengeance . . . And I plan . . . One day, a woman comes along, speaking of killing the Commodore, and my heart almost bursts with hope . . . I choose to help her . . . I choose to fight . . .*

*I choose to live . . .*

The eel's jaws never make it to my face.

My eyes snap open and a hand blurs up and seizes the predator fish by the neck, blackened fingers squeezing in a merciless grip as the eel writhes and whips its long fin, jaws snapping.

I bring the eel to my mouth and sink my fangs into it, red blooming in the water about me as I drink its blood. The eel's glowing orange eye dulls and its body slows and droops in my grip, drained of life.

And I wait. And I heal.

I do not know how long it takes. Every minute, every moment is a struggle, a titanic fight to live on. But bit by bit, my body begins to repair itself, the muscle growing back over exposed ribs, the crisped and crackling skin smoothing out, my quicksilver hair sprouting out of my scalp once more. The skeletons of fish begin to accumulate around me. A bower of bones, a charnel ground for my unlucky, would-be scavengers. As time ebbs and flows with the water, I become a strange phenomenon, down there in the deep. A slumbering enchantment. Silt and debris slow around me, congeal into a gossamer cocoon over my body. Anemones barnacle themselves to my legs. Tiny fish dart in and out of my floating cloud of hair as if it were seaweed. I have turned into a dream.

Not once do my eyes close or look away from the sun glimmering up there above the surface. I see what waits for me up there. It keeps me clinging to life, as tenacious as a pearl.

The Commodore must die. I will have my vengeance. My vengeance has become the sun.

At last, my skin glows white and perfect once more, and I feel my strength return.

It's time.

I sit up, dragging myself out of my cocoon like a part of the reef coming to life. The movement causes the pain to crash over me again in pulsing waves, but it doesn't stop me. I rip away bright scabs of starfish and limpets and encroaching formations of coral and push to my feet, take my first slow, dreamlike step. Then another. I know where I'm going. It draws me on like the sun that would give me death. There in the darkness of the deep, I lean forward to march step by agonizing step across the seafloor. A bizarre creature, a marine peculiarity. Unerring, unstoppable, indomitable as the tide, sand puffing up from my footfalls, my pale blond hair floating like a wedding veil behind me. I have no notion of how long it takes; it may be an hour, or the remaining duration of the universe. But when the seafloor finally angles up and my head emerges from that briny dream, it is night, the stars like a scattering of crushed diamonds above me.

I wipe the cold sheen of water from my face, slick my hair back from my brow and look about.

The clubhouse of the Nosferyachtu Club shines before me like a beacon.

I trudge out of the shallows and toward its lights.

I'm not sure why I think he'll be there. I'm not even sure I have a coherent plan for what to do if he is. It does not matter: all will fall into place before my implacable will.

There's an encampment of bodyguards outside the entrance to the club; the place has been turned into a fortress. At my approach, they startle and hastily lift the barrels of their tactical rifles, eyes to night vision scopes. But their commander raises an arm. "Wait," he orders, his voice low with awe. "It's the Shipwright."

And they give way before me.

When I push open the door to the throne room, every head within turns toward me.

Silence falls.

The Antisolarium of the Nosferyachtu Club hasn't changed much since I first built it for the Commodore. It's still huge and windowless, still made from the hull panels and curving beams of sailing ships I salvaged for him. More than half of the triangular personal signal flags no longer hang from the ceiling, showing how many members have perished or parted ways with the club. And there's barely a scattering of members about the room, a far cry from the hordes of supporters the Commodore enjoyed during his heyday.

But I do not care for any of that. All I have eyes for is the throne on the dais at the far end of the room. All I have eyes for is the person sitting on the throne.

My blood sings in my veins. My skin prickles with the thought of seizing the Commodore's head in my hands, burying my thumbs into those lambent eyes. Of the almost dizzying rush of vengeance after all these centuries.

But it's not the Commodore on that throne. It's not the destroyer of my life.

It's Aurora Strand.

Her back stiffens, her eyes wide as she takes in my nakedness and the seawater dripping from me onto the floor and pooling at my feet.

She opens her mouth. "Ilsa," she breathes.

# THREE

For a moment, I do not recognize that word. The noise is foreign to my ears, those ears that have not heard human speech for what seems like a lifetime.

Then I realize that I had forgotten my name.

Someone else says it. It's Adrian. His face, somehow, is tan now, though at the moment it's turning white and slack with wonder. He rushes down from the dais to halt before me, takes me in as if I'm a hallucination. "I looked for you," he says, eyes huge. "I thought—I thought you were—" Then he pulls me to him in a fierce embrace. I stand, mute as a stone, in his arms. "Thank you," he breathes. "I'm so sorry. If I hadn't—if I hadn't insisted on surfacing—" His voice catches, his broad back tightening in self-blame. Then he's pulling away, a sudden anger in his eyes. "Someone get her a towel, for goodness sake."

Someone scurries forward, and then Adrian is draping a towel around me to hide my nakedness. I do not notice, am not aware of it at all. Adrian has to take my hand and pinch my fingers into the cloth to keep it from slipping off me.

Then Arie has risen from her throne. She approaches me, her hands outheld. She's much paler than I remember her. She does not wear her yachtie clothing anymore, or her somewhat innocent style of landwear. She is draped in a stunning gold Versace dress that makes her look like a goddess among men.

I do not understand.

She holds me by the shoulders, her voice kind, elegant, almost queenly. "I cannot thank you enough for your sacrifice."

I have no time for these sentiments. They are not what's important.

I lick my salty lips and try to form words. My voice comes out as a halting croak, watery and wet and tasting of brine. "Where . . . is . . . he?"

Arie glances at Adrian, back to me, a furrow pinching her brows. "You mean Volok?"

"We have . . . to find him. We have . . . to kill him. I need . . . to see his face . . . when he dies . . ."

There's a shuffling in the throne room. Arie and Adrian exchange another look, this one uncomfortable.

Arie's thumbs rub my arms through the towel. "You've been gone for half a year, Ilsa. A lot has happened. I was successful. The Commodore has been slain. I'm the Commodore now."

I hear the words but do not hear them. A howling void has opened in my skull.

"Slain?" I manage.

Arie nods.

And I see the fangs poking out from under her upper lip now, suddenly pick up on her unmistakable scent of the undead. Hear the boom of living blood in Adrian's veins.

It's true.

There's a great bottoming out in my guts, an immense shrinking. It can't be. This can't be. What do I live for now?

The room quivers.

"Ilsa?" Adrian is frowning at me.

But it's Arie who understands. She touches his shoulder, looks into his eyes. "Let's give her a moment."

She retreats to her throne, and Adrian hesitates, his gaze lingering on me. But he reluctantly follows, taking a seat beside her. There are others here. Some I recognize from their visits to Transmarinia. Others I don't. There's a young, brash-looking blonde seated on the other side of Arie. She looks to be Arie's age, and has her flair for fashion. She watches me with an intense curiosity.

But I cannot meet their gaze. A feeling much like humiliation is burning under my skin, making my body tremble, my hand fist into the towel on my chest. I feel cheated—tricked—as if a cruel joke has been played on me.

I should be euphoric, I know. It happened. He's gone. His reign is over. I should be happy.

But I'm not.

Arie, sensing that I need reassurance and distraction, fills the throne room with her voice. "Things are different now. I have dismantled Volok's operations. Castle Volok, *The Palace of the Fang*, the Bloodhouse, the Familiar Resort—all have been shut down, all decommissioned. It is a crime now to prey on women."

But that is not enough. Not nearly enough.

"And what . . . about *me?*" I croak, beating my chest with a hand. "The rage . . . is still there." Tears, to my shame, leap to my eyes. "What do I live for . . . now that Volok . . . is gone?"

Arie watches me with sad, knowing eyes. "I don't know, Ilsa."

I lift my gaze to the ceiling, unwilling to cry in front of this audience.

"I would never ask you to be the Shipwright again," Arie goes on in a gentle tone. "But if you think it would give you purpose—"

And memory seeps back into me, reminding me of who I am, who I used to be.

Who I used to love.

"Where is he?" I croak.

Arie cocks her head, looking as if she's concerned for my sanity. "Volok is—"

"Reinhard," I say, dragging my voice closer to human speech. "My husband. He was taken from me, held hostage to keep me enslaved on Transmarinia. Volok must have hidden him somewhere . . ."

Arie studies her hands in her lap, looking uncomfortable. The blonde on her left speaks up. "Those who'd know aren't here. Arie's decisions have . . . not exactly been popular among the coven."

I glance around at the few loyalists in the shadows of the throne room. All of them, I realize, are women. "What are you saying?"

Arie lifts her head and speaks now, a hint of bitterness in her words. "It's no secret they're not thrilled to have a woman as Commodore. There's already been an assassination attempt on my life." Adrian's knuckles whiten on his thighs, and Arie gives him a sympathetic look. "And some have openly defied my laws and preyed on women. Those caught have been punished, but my reign is . . . under threat. Volok may be dead, but there are pockets of rebels still loyal to him. His boat, the *Keep*, disappeared the day I was named Commodore. I believe the leader of these cultists commands it. And that he's developing a plan to remove me from the throne." She lets out a long, weary sigh. "I'm sorry. But everyone from that time who'd know is either dead or turned traitor."

My head feels too sluggish, too waterlogged to take this in. But more memories suck and pull at me like tide, revealing glittering finds amongst the murk.

I lift my chin. "I think I know of someone from that time who would."

Shared looks amongst the court. "Who?"

"Volok's first blood son. He held no love for the Russian. He led a rebellion against him, in the early days of his reign. It was foiled, and the blood son was caught and punished, buried in an iron coffin at the bottom of the sea. In a place called the Hole of Souls."

Even the name brings a chill to my skin. Arie and Adrian seem to share it—they glance at each other, uneasy. "You know where this place is?"

I shake my head. "No. But its location can be found in an atlas kept in the archives of Volok's castle."

Arie looks uncomfortable again. "Castle Volok has been sunken."

"That won't stop me."

The new Commodore studies me, a small smile curling the edges of her mouth. "No, I believe it won't." The smile fades. "But it's not safe to go there. The castle has become a pilgrimage site for Volok's cultists. You'll need protection."

I open my mouth to object.

"I insist," Arie says, her voice brooking no argument. "These are dangerous times. Many vampires who were turned back into men when Volok died were asked to be bitten again; there are more cultists every day. And you'll need a captain." She takes Adrian's hand in hers, a tenderness easing her face. "I know of someone. He's ex-military. An old body guard who helped me sort out pockets of resistance in the early days and saved me from my assassination attempt. I can think of no one I would trust more to protect you." She pauses. "Besides. If you insist on doing this, then I must ask that you find out how the cultists are planning to supplant me. You'll need help for that."

I bow my head. "Thank you, Commodore."

Arie's eyes crinkle at my formality. "I would go with you, but I am needed here. So please, stay awhile. You need rest. And time with friends."

My lips twitch, my face trying to remember what it's like to smile. "You will always be my friend, Aurora Strand," I answer, my heart clenching. "But I have waited long enough."

Arie shares a small smile with Adrian, and I know she's thinking of everything she did for him. All the ways she fought for her love.

She returns her gaze to me. "I understand."

Silence falls in the throne room. Adrian studies me, worry pinching the seams of his mouth. "These cultists," he says at last. "They call themselves the Sons of Volok. You will know them by their ensign." He turns to the blonde on Arie's other side. "Cailee?"

The young woman nods and rises from her chair, hands pinching the corners of a vast sheet of cloth—the thing they'd all been discussing when I arrived. It drops in a liquid unfurling to reveal a black banner scrawled with a jagged green V that seems to glow with uncanny light. The sight makes my flesh creep.

Adrian's eyes never leave me. "If you see a boat flying that flag? You run. Understand?"

A shudder passes through me, and I nod.

Adrian's head inclines in satisfaction. "Good luck, Ilsa," he says, his kindness almost stern in its intensity. "I hope you find your husband."

# FOUR

They call Florida the Sunshine State for good reason.

The light seems to permeate everything: the waving fronds of palm trees, the heat-blurred asphalt, the glowing Atlantic. It burns into my mind like radiation. My sunglasses and the tinted windows of my rental car don't seem to do a thing. Within ten minutes of driving, a pounding migraine has set in; an hour in and I'm ready to tear apart the first hitchhiker who crosses my path.

I can't help but be fascinated by Florida, though. I've never visited the States, never set foot on land outside of Germany and Sanguisuga. And the Florida Keys have their own unique charm. The Seven Mile Bridge connecting the mainland to the Keys is exhilarating, a stretch of overseas highway that seems to glide on forever through the sky. Then a leapfrogging of bridges connecting one key to another, and dense tunnels through kudzu jungle broken up by funky tiki bars with outlandish signs, thatched oceanfront roadhouses that serve daiquiris and conch fritters and key lime pie.

I keep an eye out for the green and white mile markers along the highway, glancing now and then at the scrap of paper Arie gave me as if the address will change on me: *Diver's Den, MM119, Sundown Key.*

I wonder what this friend of Arie's will be like. I don't have much faith in the kind of man who'd choose to end up down here. The Keys, with their crocodiles and backwater rednecks and spooky stories of haunted shipwrecks, don't exactly scream professionalism.

I brush a piece of lint from my lap. The first thing I'd done after my startling entrance in Arie's court was purchase a new business suit—gray with high-waisted, flared pants—and I feel more myself again. My snack this afternoon helped, too. I had ended up picking up a hitchhiker. In deference to Arie's new laws, I'd chosen a male criminal. A boozy ex-con breaking parole who'd been picking fights in the parking lot of a bar in Key Largo. I'd lured him into the rental car with the promise of a roadside quickie. I didn't lie—it had indeed been quick, though not with the kind of penetration he'd been expecting. He jigged in the grip of my fangs for less than a minute, his eyes rolling back as the life drained out of him. I didn't spill a single drop of blood.

I dropped off the body around mile marker 96, shoving it out into the throbbing sunlight with enough force to roll it into the kudzu. Then I'd wiped my mouth and driven on without a backward glance.

The entire time, I'd imagined he was Volok. Or Reinhard's captors.

It barely scratched the itch of my anger.

The afternoon grows long, and the sun is dipping toward the horizon by the time I cross a bridge into Sundown Key.

This key is the most dilapidated I've seen thus far. Overgrown and ravaged by hurricanes, its signs muddied and dented with buckshot. Here and there, glimpses of abandoned, haunted-looking waterfront villas, collapsed houses, the rusting hulks of cars along the roadways.

Mile marker 119 glides into view.

There's a turnoff after it. A washed-out road winding into the jungle.

I take it.

I have serious misgivings at this point. I wonder if Arie made a mistake. If she wrote down the wrong mile marker. Surely a man she trusted with her life wouldn't live out here.

The road straightens out and the jungle opens up. I can see the sparkle of the Gulf of Mexico. A private beach. Before it stands a shack of a bungalow. Old and leaning, its roof tiles askew, half of them blown off by a recent hurricane. Beside it an Airstream propped up on concrete blocks, its aluminum coachwork dented and banged up by hundreds of thousands of miles of travel.

I park the rental car and sit there, feeling unease coil in my gut as I study the yard. There's a motorcycle in the drive, its engine block gone, its tension chain off. In the tall grass the overturned hulls of rowboats, a graveyard of rusting boat parts.

This is a waste of time.

I pull on black leather gloves and open the driver side door, unfurl a black umbrella and angle it to shield my face as I step out, feeling the golden rays of dusk baking into its canopy like the heat of an oven. My ankle wobbles, the heels of my black leather business boots sinking into the mud. I feel ridiculous and completely out of place here.

I manage to navigate the front yard, though, avoiding the rusting relics in the grass. The porch boards of the bungalow creak under my feet. I rap the crooked screen-door with my fist, expecting it to fall off.

"Herr Kalawai'a?"

No answer. The knock echoes sad and forlorn inside the bungalow. I'm considering knocking on the Airstream when I hear the high whine of an electric tool.

It's coming from the beach behind the bungalow.

There's a verandah surrounding the shack. I circle it, noting the wetsuits and scuba gear draped over its railing to dry in the sun, the oxygen tanks and spearguns leaned against it.

On the beach, there's a ramshackle private dock, a boat lift attached to its end. The lift is holding what looks like a shipwreck out of the water. It's an ancient 40-foot sportfisher yacht, its brightwork mottled red with rust, its gelcoat spiderwebbed with stress cracks, its steel hull covered in marine growths, its wood paneling seemingly made from the same timber as the shack and in dire need of a fresh paint of polyurethane. It's a travesty.

I see now what the whine is coming from. It's a stick welder, as I thought. A flux shielded arc with a 2.5 mm rod, by the looks of it. A man is using it to patch the hull with a steel plate, the spray of sparks leaping from his arc reflected in the eye shield of his welder's helmet. He's burly, the well-used coveralls he's wearing straining over huge curves of muscle, one knee resting on a wooden pallet.

But it's his work I'm more focused on.

"You're doing it wrong," I call, getting close.

He doesn't hear me over the spit and crackle of his welder, so I take a step closer.

"YOU'RE DOING IT WRONG!"

This gets his attention. The sparks die as he switches off the electrode. Then he's standing and pulling off his welder's helmet, shaking loose a shaggy mane of swingy dark hair with glints of gold in it. It's magnificent.

So is his face.

It's long, tanned, strong-cheeked, clearly Hawaiian, with a kingly beard. The face of a lion. It frowns at me, thick eyebrows drawing down in confusion. "What's that?"

His voice is deep and growly. Even his heartbeat is slow and strong.

Then his scent hits me.

Everything recedes.

The hitchhiker this afternoon should have been enough to tide me over for a few days. His blood, though, had tasted like tar. Rancid. Soused in liquor.

Nose-wrinklingly bad. Nothing like what this man's blood must taste like.

Suddenly my mouth is watering.

"You're doing it wrong," I say again, trying to still the waver in my voice.

He looks me up and down, taking in my pantsuit, my umbrella and sunglasses, and his lips draw back in a blinding smile that ruins all the fierceness in that face. "You must be the Shipwright."

I blink. No one has ever dismissed my advice before. I tighten my grip on my umbrella. "The quality of that weld is bad," I persist, nostrils flaring as I point at his work. "You're going to have to grind it out and re-weld it."

His smile turns rakish. "She'll hold, thanks." He sets down his arc and helmet on the pallet, offers a huge hand. "Kaipo."

At a loss, I take it. It's strong. Very warm. Full of blood.

I swallow. "Ilsa." Then: "Really, if you don't re-weld it—"

He looks me in the eye. "A weld can be good without it looking good." Then he's winked and clapped me on the arm, turned away to unbutton his coveralls.

My jaw hangs. *Who does he think he—*

But I'm distracted by him shrugging the top half of his coveralls off and letting it hang from his waist, revealing that he's wearing nothing beneath. The shock of all that skin stops the words in my throat. His back is as wide as a barnyard door, muscles sheathing his body like steel. And they're covered in all-over tribal tattoos, a whorling of black geometric designs crosshatched with old spearfishing scars. He practically throbs with life.

He leans over a washbasin by the verandah and splashes his face with water, grabs a cloth to dab himself dry. It's as if he's splashed me in the face.

Finding my anger again, I stalk after him. "You always ignore people with hundreds of years more experience than you?"

"Only when they're arrogant." He tosses the cloth aside and turns about to face me, his upper body swinging as lithe as a swimmer's. "You always insult people you need help from?"

I open my mouth, ready to breathe fire, and catch the small grin teasing the corner of his mouth.

He's playing with me.

I drop my shoulders, eyes hooded and determined to not let him get to me. "Arie—the Commodore—told you why I've come, then?"

He crosses his burly arms over the wide shelves of his pecs and waits.

He's really going to make me ask for it.

I let out a loud sigh. "Will you help me?" I lower my voice. "Please?"

He rubs his chin. "Risk my life guarding an arrogant immortal from a pack of bloodthirsty monsters?" He cocks his head, eyes slitted as he thinks it over—then his face breaks into a boyish grin. "Why not." He claps his hands and gestures behind me. "I'll just need a few days to make the *Kanaloa* seaworthy."

It takes a moment for it to set in. Then my eyes bug as I glance back at the wreck of a sportfishing yacht. "*That?* You want to use—" I let out a snort of a laugh. "No. We're not using that hunk of junk—"

That lion's face grows fierce again. "You may know how to build a boat," he says, nettled. "But do you know how to pilot one? Are you trained in combat situations? No?"

I cross my arms over my chest, too proud to admit that I don't and I'm not.

He jerks his head down once in a nod. "Then it would appear you need me. And my hunk of junk boat." He walks past me to place a hand to her hull. "None of these cultists would suspect a sportfishing yacht. She'll blend right in."

I scowl. This will probably be the stupidest mistake of my life. This man seems like more of a surfer bro than a mercenary. But I don't have the luxury of turning him down. I have a terrible feeling I'm running out of time, and I can't bear to wait much longer.

Reinhard needs me.

"Fine. You have two days to get her ready. Though I doubt two years would be enough."

Kaipo Kalawai'a turns back to me as the sun sets behind the *Kanaloa*, bathing the bungalow and the palm trees of Sundown Key in a red glare. "Where are you going?"

I lower my umbrella, collapsing its canopy so I can let it hang at my side.

I lift my chin to face him. "To see a friend of a friend."

# FIVE

I catch a red eye to Colorado and spend the following day holed up in a hotel near the airport. I black out the room by drawing the blinds, scotch taping their edges to the walls to block out every trace of light. Then I collapse on the bed and fall into a deep, deep sleep.

I dream of Reinhard. I dream of Volok keeping him chained in some dark cell, feeding him just enough blood to keep him alive. I think of him emaciated, filthy, bags under his eyes, holding yellow-nailed hands to his face as he weeps in a corner. I dream of him calling my name in his sleep.

I wake with his name on my lips.

When dark falls, I pick up my rental car—an SUV with 4-wheel drive and winter tires—and drive up into the Rockies.

It's not long before I hit the snows. They're deep, clumping up the trees and blanketing the peaks in a heavy dumping of white. I have to stop to put chains on the tires. Then the SUV is sweeping along the curves of the mountains, switchbacking higher and higher until I can see the vast tableland of Colorado below. Even with my unnaturally sharp eyes, I can barely see ten feet in front of me; the beams of the SUV whirl with snow.

I wonder why anyone would live out here. And then I wonder if they went far enough to get away from yachting and all its horrors.

The gloom deepens. Gentle, goose-feather flakes rush down out of the dark to blot up the windshield and get struck down by the wipers. The boughs of the pines crowd in above me, turning the road into a close, dark, narrow corridor. More and more, the SUV struggles and fishtails through the rising snowfall, and I wonder if I'll get stuck out here, will have to walk the rest of the way.

Then I see the lights of the mansion up ahead.

The house looks like an alpine ski lodge, made of rock wall facades and an exposed timber frame. Drifts of snow have accumulated against it, its eaves hung with icicles, dustings of powder whipping off its roof in the storm. A perfect hideaway spot for a family.

When I knock on the door, I hear the shout of the family's gruff protector and am greeted by the barrel of a tactical shotgun.

I don't have time for that.

I step across the threshold and pull back the fur-trimmed hood of my parka to reveal myself, my long sheet of pale blond hair whipping in the skirling winds about me.

I part my full red lips. "No need for that, Herr Redfearn."

It takes a while for the surprise and nerves to leave the former captain of Adrian's yacht. Arnold Redfearn sits across from me on a couch in the living room. On his right, his former chief stewardess, the woman I had known for years as Mrs. Colding and who is now his wife. On his left, his daughter. They all hold guns in their laps or stand them beside them. They are a family of survivors.

I can respect that.

I tell them everything. How I survived the explosion. My slumber at the bottom of the sea. Marching out of the water to look for Volok. And now my quest to find my husband the former Commodore took from me. And why I need to start with the atlas in Castle Volok.

When I'm done, Redfearn sits in silence for a long moment. He's grown out his stubble into a silver beard, and he absently strokes it, his eyes unfocused, lost in the middle distance. Then he rises and marches to the fireplace. There's a small box on the mantel. Black, unadorned. He lifts the lid and takes out what's inside, brings it to me. He holds it out.

It's a scrap of paper. Nothing on it but a list of numbers.

They're coordinates. For the location of Castle Volok.

"I don't envy you going into that place."

"No," I say, a shiver taking me as I fold up the paper and tuck it into a parka pocket. "I don't, either." I meet his eyes. "But thank you."

He rests his hands on his hips. His plaid coat had been dusted with snow when I arrived, and it now gleams wet with melted flakes. He must have been outside collecting firewood.

His face is very serious.

"I should be thanking you," he says.

I blink at him.

"You sacrificed a lot. For Arie. For her cause." He thumbs his nose, not seeming to know where to look, or how to say this. But he makes a valiant attempt. "That woman means a helluva lot to me. More than you know." At last, he finds my gaze, and the full force of it is like a shock to my system. "So thank you, Ilsa."

I open my mouth. My heart has lodged in my throat.

"You're welcome, Herr Redfearn."

The ex-captain bobs his head, his ears pink, and glances at his family. They are beaming with gentle pride.

He harrumphs deep in his throat. "You said it's not over." When I frown at him, he adds, "That there are cultists out there. That Arie's in danger."

I nod.

"And you'll do the best you can to help her."

He's looking for a promise, I know. My word that I'll do everything I can to help his friend. Our friend.

So I give it: "I will."

He nods at that, a small part of him satisfied. But he's still wrestling with guilt.

"I'm sorry, but I can't go with you," he tells me. "My days of skippering are over." He glances at the faces of his wife and daughter. They look back at him, eyes shining. "I have a family now. I can't risk that."

I give a twitch of my lips in acknowledgment, feeling a twinge of jealousy and hating myself for it. The least I can do is absolve him of his guilt. "I wouldn't want you to," I assure him. "Don't worry—Arie put me in touch with someone."

Mrs. Colding—*Mrs. Redfearn*—arches a brow. "Who?"

I shrug. "I don't know, I just met him. He's ex-military."

This makes Redfearn's flushed ears perk up. "He should know what he's doing, then." His eyes narrow at me with fatherly protectiveness. "What do you think of him?"

I take a moment, seeing Kaipo with his boyish flash of teeth and scrap heap of a boat, that infuriating arrogance that stirs something in me I can't quite name. "Besides being insufferable?" I snort. "I'm not sure yet." I drag my thoughts away from that mystery and lift my eyes to the Redfearn family. "Arie wanted me to check in on you, though. See how her favorite family is doing."

This changes Redfearn's face, that graveness giving way to pride and joy. He reaches out and takes his wife's hand, and there's no mistaking the look in her eyes as she looks up at him, her thumb brushing the backs of his knuckles. He smiles. "We're doing well."

I can't help it: My heart aches. I hastily try to cover it up and look over at the young woman on the couch. "I see you found your daughter."

Penelope Redfearn blushes and flicks a glance at her father. His face is gentle with love and relief. "I did."

There's a prickling behind my eyes now. Mortified, I clear my throat and try to blink it away. "I'm happy for you, Arnold."

Redfearn rests his gaze on me, and it is sorrowful and full of an unbearable empathy and understanding. "I hope you find the one you love, Ilsa. I really do."

I try to smile for them, a painful twisting of my lips. I am looking at them but I'm not seeing them. Everything is blurred-up firelight and grief and outrage at the universe that I am alone, have been alone for so long, maybe will be alone forever.

# SIX

As soon as I'm back, I'm immediately reminded of why Kaipo Kalawai'a is absolutely infuriating.

"I don't understand why we can't just fly to China and rent a boat there," I grumble as I look out before us. "We're wasting so much time."

"This is my baby," he huffs, sounding insulted. "Besides, I'd have to get used to handling a new boat. I already know the *Kanaloa*. And if your hubby survived a couple of centuries as a hostage, he'll survive a couple more weeks."

I scowl. We're standing on the skeletal tuna tower, an aluminum and stainless-steel platform mounted on the *Kanaloa*'s superstructure that's mainly used for spotting fish. But it also has a second control station, which Kaipo is taking full advantage of now.

He eases forward on the throttle. It's early morning in the Port of Miami, and we're waiting to board a yacht transport for the transpacific crossing to China. The carrier is like nothing I've ever seen—it's a behemoth, seemingly miles long and wide enough to fit three yachts across, its red hull lurid in the dawn glow of Florida.

And we'll be trapped on it for two weeks.

The idea already has me feeling green around the gills.

I adjust the angle of my umbrella resting on my shoulder. The tuna tower's sunshade cover isn't doing much at this hour, and so my pantsuit, gloves, sunglasses and umbrella have to do today. I already have a splitting headache.

"Ready?" Kaipo asks.

It's our turn now. The carrier's great door has lowered to flood the cargo bay and turn it into a boat basin. Over two dozen oncoming yachts have already floated inside, packed as tight as sardines, like a snapshot of rush hour traffic.

Kaipo, I have to hand it to him, is a damn good pilot. He slides the *Kanaloa* as smooth as butter into our predetermined position, a narrow slot right in front of the carrier's port stern stack that's so snug against the carrier's hull our fenders squeak. Then the crew are tossing him heavy-duty orange straps which he feeds through the hawseholes, around the bollards, and out again where they're ratcheted tight, keeping the yacht in place.

I hear splashing and join Kaipo at the gunwale. There are divers in the water placing supports under our boat. Before long, there's a clunk and the millions of gallons of water in the carrier begins to get pumped out. It's so slow it's almost imperceptible—only the gold plimsoll or draft marks on the starboard quarter, marked in ascending order in meters, prove that anything is happening. But by and by the water finally drains, leaving all the yachts high and dry on chocks over a rust-colored deck ten or fifteen feet below, the sensation eerie and unearthly.

This is our home now.

"Ready to take a tour?"

Kaipo leads me astern. As he strides down the gangway, he lifts a hand and calls out to a couple of riders on neighboring boats as they fasten down cargo or attach fittings to water hoses. When they look up and see him, their faces split into huge grins. "Fishman!" they call. "Who's the lady friend?"

He waves them off, laughing. They all seem to know him. And they all love him.

A strange, unsettling feeling twists at my guts.

"You know the tuna tower," he says, gesturing aloft to the aluminum tower, and then the deck below it. "And the wheelhouse." I do know it. It had been cramped, the wood paneling warped and stained, its wheel worn smooth and cracked in places. Hardly encouraging.

Then we're in the fishing cockpit at the stern with its racks of harpoons and spearguns and its array of fishing rods stuck into a clamp-on fishing arch. "And this is my beauty." He grips the back of a squeaky swivel fighting chair bolted to the deck and swings it about. It's an old, worn thing with a teak seat and footrest, chrome-plated brass gimbals for freedom of movement and a holder for fishing poles. He runs a loving hand along the crown of the seat. "I've caught a lot of giants in this baby."

After a moment, he seems to come to himself. "Now for inside." He winks at me and hauls back the door to the main cabin in a squeaking of rusty tracks and we're inside the *Kanaloa.*

Inside his world.

It's chaos. "Don't mind the mess," he casually remarks as he steps over boat parts laid out on tarps. There's a sectional couch here, a flatscreen TV hanging askew in a dusty wood entertainment system. Beyond, a bar and galley, the fridge ancient, the barstools dinged-up and sad-looking. Parts of the floor are even torn up to reveal bare plywood beneath. She looks like a deathtrap.

I must have a look on my face, because Kaipo holds up his hands. "Hey, she'll clean up. This is where the guests will hang out. They can watch the Marlins on TV while their buddies catch a marlin outside."

Dubious, I collapse my umbrella and tuck it under one arm. "You want to do charters, then?"

He shrugs. "South Florida has become a 'roided-out Mediterranean. Everyone wants to do day charters here. You know, time-crunched celebs willing to drop fifteen grand on a joyride." A slight sullenness enters his voice. "They claim it's for the fishing, but really they just wanna drop anchor on a sandbar off Key Biscayne and play with the toys and girls before they're too drunk, then dock at the trendiest club."

I snort. "What a noble profession."

He gives me a look, something glinting behind that happy-go-lucky attitude. "But that's not who I'll be doing it for. I'll be doing it for those like me. Who love fishing for what it is. And when I get too old for chartering, I'll retire and live out my days on a beach in Cozumel."

Cozumel. The name gleams in the air, as rare and golden as a fairy tale. It unsettles my doubt. "You like fishing that much?"

An infectious grin splits his beard. "I live for it. Mahi, sailfish, tuna, white marlin, sharks. I do it all, sweetheart."

I stop myself from rolling my eyes, doubt firmly back in place.

Yup. Surfer bro all the way.

Next is a rickety wooden staircase leading us below deck. He shoves open a metal door and a blast of furnace heat hits us. "The engine room."

It's filthy. The shine on the diamond plate flooring bisecting the engines has been scuffed up with scratches, and the high-gloss white paint everywhere that's meant to reflect light has been dulled by oil stains and grime. "Two thousand horsepower," he brags. "She can get up and move." He lovingly taps a bulkhead and one of the lights flickers and goes off. He coughs, bangs the bulkhead again and the light flickers back on. He smiles. "Shall we?"

"Guest cabins." He gestures to a series of staterooms packed to the brim with tools and materials and spare parts. "And master cabin."

I peek in, curious despite myself. It's bigger than the others, full-beam but with only the basics: a bed long enough for his frame, a closet with a wetsuit hanging on the door. On the nightstand a copy of Hemingway's *The Old Man and the Sea*. He really is a cliché.

"This is where we'll, uh, be sleeping," he announces.

My spine goes rigid. "I'm sorry." I turn to him, eyes closed and voice deadly soft. "I must have misheard. Where we'll be *what?*"

He holds up his hands. "I'm sorry, but you saw the guest cabins. I know the *Kanaloa* needs some work—"

"Some?" I scoff. "Ha!"

"*Buuuuut*," he says, pumping his hands. "I'm gonna use the transport time as a mini yard period. Get her shipshape to find your hubby. And once everything is out of one of the guest cabins, you can move—"

I drop my chin down to give him a dead-eyed look. "In time for—" I shake my head, amazed. "There's no way—"

"No way," he agrees, nodding sagely. Then he strokes his beard, a mischievous glint in his eyes. "Unless, of course, the Shipwright of Transmarinia helps me."

I stare at him in the bowels of that rinky-dink sportfishing yacht, equally outraged and impressed.

*This motherfucker.*

"I don't know who you think you are," I snarl. "But I'm married. I am *not* going to sleep in the same bed as—"

"And you won't," he assures me. "I mean, not at the same time, anyway."

I cross my arms, head cocked.

"Your kind prefers to sleep during the day, right? You're tired then, and I know all the light for you is painful . . ."

I rub my pounding forehead. "Don't remind me."

"So we'll take turns. I work during the day and sleep at night, and you sleep during the day and work at night. We'll have completely opposite schedules. You'll barely see me. You can avoid me all you want. Which, I'm getting the vibe, *is* what you want. Right?"

I tap my foot, looking for something to object to and not finding it.

A slow grin creeps up the side of his mouth, and he lifts a brow. "Well?" He squares off with me, and I look down to see he's offering a hand. "Deal?"

After a long moment, I sigh and take it.

*Goddamn it.*

# SEVEN

I wake feeling more rested than I have in a while. Yes, I had quite the rest at the bottom of the sea, but there had been nothing restful about it—that had been a fight for survival. This, though? This is decadent. This is peaceful. This is—

Kaipo's bed.

My body stiffens. I'd fallen asleep at once after our conversation. Kaipo had blacked out the windows with roll-down shutters, turning the cabin as dark as the earth. And the bed is much softer than I thought it would be. The pillows fluffy. The comforter thick and warm. And the smell is nice, both alluring and comforting. What is that? A musk of sea brine, beard oil and man.

Oh.

Kaipo's scent.

My face grows hot.

I pull on my pantsuit and shuffle out into the yacht, rubbing at my eyes. It's night, Kaipo nowhere to be seen. When I pull back the sliding glass door leading out onto the fishing cockpit at the stern, I see that we're at sea, the white fleck of froth spread out for miles behind us, stars wheeling overhead. Kaipo watches it all from his fighting chair, beer in hand.

The chair squeaks as he shifts to grin at me. "Morning, Shipwright."

I grunt as I come to stand beside him, arms crossed at the night chill. "You always have to be so happy?"

A small grin lights his eyes. "Humor isn't your strong suit, is it?"

I scowl. "I'm German. We don't do humor."

Unflappable, he offers a bottle. "Beer?"

I wrinkle my nose. "Not my liquid of choice." I glance around. It's odd seeing so many other boats around us, all suspended in the air in a hum of polyester straps, cradles propped beneath them. Other boat owners are out on deck, too. Eating, drinking, sneaking a cigarette in orange glows of burning tobacco. A gentle bustle of life.

A lot of blood.

I swallow, mouth watering, and lean over the gunwale to look toward the bow of the carrier, my pale blond hair whipping in the wind off the sea. Above the shapes of the docked boats, all I can see is the black wall of the carrier's bridge and living area superstructure, broken up by blinking navigation lights, a few glowing windows.

"Where are we?" I ask.

Kaipo shrugs. "Not sure." He takes a swig of his beer and sucks his teeth. "We're headed toward Golfito, where we'll pass through the Panama Canal, go up the West Coast and then make the crossing to China."

Impatience gnaws at me again. "We better make sure your old lady is ready, then." I pace in front of him, hugging myself. "I'll do a full inspection of the *Kanaloa* tonight and draw up a checklist of refit tasks. I'll divvy them up between us according to our skills. You know how to weld. Sort of. Can you do electrical?"

He smiles to himself as he rests his beer on his thigh, turning it so that its glass catches the moonlight. "Sort of."

"Carpentry?"

He nods.

"Plumbing?"

He shrugs.

"Engineering?"

He waggles a hand in the air: *Passable*.

"All right." I nod, mentally tallying up the workload. "I'll work on the more mechanical side of things. You'll get the more—physical stuff."

When I glance at Kaipo, his beard is twitched in a smirk.

"What?" I say, feeling suddenly self-conscious.

He scrapes a nail at the label of his beer, shrugs his barn door shoulders. "Nothing. Just . . . you always like this with your crew back in Transmarinia?"

I arch a brow. "Meaning?"

He muses on the right words. "Exacting. Untrusting. Angry."

I snort at that, tuck a sleek sheet of fair hair out of my face. "I'm always angry."

I can feel his eyes on me. "Why's that?"

Images flash through my mind—Reinhard's face, Volok lifting a long icicle finger to his lips to shush my screams, blood spreading in a tide through drifts of sawdust while rats suffocate me with their hairy little bodies—and it's too much.

"What about you?" I ask, turning to him with arms crossed. "How did you fall in with Arie?"

He studies me, a small smile playing about his lips that tells me he knows what I just did. But he rolls with it. "I already knew about her kind. Many do in the yachting industry. So when I heard of her rise to power and how she wanted to change things, I was all in."

I nod and toe the deck, my voice lowering to something approaching respect. "She mentioned you saved her from assassination."

He stares at me a moment as if debating something, the humor on his face frozen, then tugs at his shirt. The top three buttons are undone, so it pulls aside easily to show a brawny swelling of pectoral. Three long, ugly snaggles of silver there that don't look like spearfishing scars.

Claw marks.

He lifts his chin. "I got lucky."

I swallow, and he tugs his shirt back into place. "Arie and Adrian were so grateful, they gave me enough money to retire ten times over. So when the worst of the danger had passed, I decided to make a go of my dream of living out my days as a fisherman. Though it sounds like that danger is starting to return." He lifts his eyes to mine, an uncharacteristic seriousness taking over his face. "I answered your question. You still haven't answered mine."

I stare at him, thinking of stricken faces and screeching rats and icicle fingers lifted to cold lips, and turn away. "Get some sleep," I order, striding past him. "We start tomorrow."

It's a moment before his answer floats after me. "Aye, aye, Shipwright."

Upon a full inspection, the *Kanaloa* is in even shockingly worse shape than I thought, which is saying something. Kaipo apparently subscribes to the spit-and-baling wire style of repairs: fishing hooks for shear pins, wine corks for springs, house wire for hose clamps. By the time I'm done, I don't bat an eye at the wads of pink bubblegum plugging up hydraulic oil leaks.

It's a miracle she still floats.

By the time a faint light along the horizon is threatening sunrise, I've finished the checklist. It's intimidatingly long and split into two columns with our names above them, a line drawn down the middle. I pin it to the galley fridge with a sailfish magnet and turn for the stairs going below deck.

That's where I bump into Kaipo.

I freeze on the top step, my pulse flickering. He's pulling a white undershirt on, and that scent of his is wafting off him, his heartbeat still slow from sleep. It flutters when he sees me.

"Shipwright," he says, tipping two fingers to his forehead in mock salute.

That nickname the neighboring riders called him comes back to me. "Fishman."

He cracks a grin. "Checklist done?"

I nod.

"I'll let you know how it goes, then."

He blinks at me, and it takes me a moment to realize he's waiting for me to get out of the way. "Oh," I say, my ears hot. I step aside and we edge around each other, his bulk almost taking up the entire stairway. I am very aware of his arm brushing my breast as he passes.

When I step into the master cabin, a pair of shorts and one of his oversized shirts is waiting for me, folded at the foot of the bed. A note atop them: *You'll need these. Can't get dirty with the rest of us in that Shipwright uniform.*

A scowl twists my mouth. I hate it, but he's right. In all my haste to get going, I had completely forgotten to bring any extra sets of clothes, and this pantsuit won't do for refit work. My days of designing yachts are over.

Tentatively, I bring his shirt to my face, close my eyes and breathe in.

When I pull the clothes on, I push down any feelings of guilt, any feelings of compromise and belonging. I can buy more clothes once we reach land. This will have to do for now.

I slip into bed, and it's still warm from his body. I pull the comforter to my chin and shut my eyes, that scent of brine and beard oil and man everywhere around me. I'm almost asleep before it comes to me that I've never felt so safe.

We start knocking off items on the refit list. He blasts the barnacles and mussels and green algae stains off the *Kanaloa*'s bottom and repaints her with antifouling, begins renovating the main cabin floor with fresh teak boards. For my part, I work like a madwoman to empty out the staterooms as quickly as I can. I replace the fuel injectors, turbochargers, water pumps and propeller blades. I change zincs. I check hydraulic hoses and work on the bow thruster. I service the generators and the a/v system. It's been a long time since I've gotten my hands this dirty, but there is a satisfaction in it. The knowledge that my work is honoring my relationship with Reinhard. That with every replacement, every passing day, I am getting that much closer to him.

Every sunrise and sunset, Kaipo and I pass each other on the stairs going below deck, our bodies brushing against each other as we change shifts, and in my mind I see Reinhard and I passing each other in our old shop.

Every night, I find a new item crossed off on the list on the fridge.

We dock in Golfito, then La Paz and Ensenada in Baja California. And every time, I sneak off into port at night and find some unwary soul on which to feed.

During these times, I do not restrain my anger.

Kaipo gets fed by the ship. Three square meals a day in the crew mess. He's popular amongst the crew and other designated yacht riders. Beloved, even.

Sometimes I'll feel his low voice vibrating through the hull. Joshing jokes. Companionable storytelling. His deep, infectious chuckle of a laugh. And, more rarely, hushed conversations. Once, memorably, as I found it hard to sleep during midday, I heard one of his rider neighbors pose a question as they drank beer above deck. "Who's your lady friend, then?"

I went stiff as a board in bed.

Kaipo played it cool. "Who?"

Snickerings of several men. "You know who. Your nocturnal companion."

"Oh, hush."

More laughter. "Seems our Fishman caught himself a special one this time. Look at him blush."

I'd lain in bed a long time after that, my heart in my throat.

One night soon after, Kaipo knocks on my door after sunset. He never does that.

"Yes?" I ask, opening the door a wary crack.

He flashes a smile. Behind him, above him, I can hear music, the roars of laughter. He jerks a thumb over his shoulder. "The fellas are having a barbecue on deck. Thought you might want to come. Show your face."

I stare at him. "My face?"

He swallows. "I mean, they've been asking about ya. Might be smart to socialize a bit. Put a stop to all the rumors."

My stomach tightens. "What rumors?"

He lets out a nervous laugh, runs a hand through his glinting mane of hair. "They all think I've got some poor girl tied up in here." His eyes fall for a moment. "And I wouldn't mind. That is, I'd like you to come."

He's wearing, I notice, a fresh polo with its top three buttons undone. A sharktooth necklace hangs down into that neckline between the glistening planes of his pecs. I can sense the warmth there—the beating life—the blood—and his scent coils into my nostrils.

All those bodies out there, all that temptation.

I take a step back. "I don't think that would be a good idea."

Hurt flashes in his eyes, but he covers it well. "Sure," he says, tapping the doorframe. "Of course. Sleep well."

I don't fall asleep for hours, listening to the hum of music and laughter of that party.

# EIGHT

One night, I wake to find we've docked in Hawaii. And none too soon—I'm ravenous, my body throbbing with hunger. I go out onto the stern to slip off into port and hunt, expecting to find Kaipo gone, off to party ashore or go night spearfishing.

But he's not. He stands with hands braced on the rail, staring out at Honolulu with its resorts and palm trees and the volcanoes of Oahu rising in the dark beyond.

I don't know how to read the expression on his face. Uncertain? Wistful? Almost . . . haunted?

Whatever mood he's in, he pulls himself out of it when he sees me, a small, halfhearted smile on his face. An acknowledgment of what I'm about to do.

I hesitate. "You're not going ashore? I thought you grew up here."

He glances off at the twinkling lights in the harbor. "Maybe later." Then, back at me: "Have a good night."

I think on him as I go ashore, not knowing what to make of his sudden seriousness.

I'm soon distracted by the pulse of life around me.

I almost envy Kaipo's childhood: Hawaii would have been a beautiful place to grow up in. It's all lights and shows, grass-skirted dancers garlanded in flowers and bare-chested warriors twirling blazing batons into blurs of roaring light. The smells waft over me: Polynesian feasts of kalua pork, taro rolls and grilled pineapple. And all the scents of blood of thousands of people.

Not far from the harbor, I find a beach park with a homeless encampment amongst a stand of dwarf palms. A huddle of tents surrounded by an overflow of trash, cooler boxes, bikes and lines of laundry flapping in the wind.

The tents suck and rustle in the night. I unzip one and peer inside.

A filthy man shivering in a sleeping bag rolls over at the sound. When he sees me, his eyes widen to the whites, his mouth gaping into a gummy hole. "You," he breathes. "You've come for me?"

I hold a finger to my lips. "Not yet." I fold a hundred-dollar bill into his shaking hand and squeeze gently. "But here's a taste."

And I tip his head to the side and groove my fangs into his neck.

He lies there, eyes wide as those of a clairvoyant, as I drink my fill.

Some of my kind can't help themselves. Once they start feeding, they're unable to stop until the victim is dead.

But my willpower is not like most of my kind.

I suckle, as delicate as a bat, until the color has started to drain from the man's face. I leave him thinking he's seen the angel of death. Maybe he has.

I know I will be for my enemies.

I think of staying out late exploring the city. There's a part of me that yearns to be among humanity again. To recover what was lost, down there in the sea.

But I go back to the ship. Maybe I'm afraid that if I break this isolation, I'll become distracted, lose my focus on my mission.

Maybe I'm thinking of Kaipo.

He's not on the boat, though. When I return to the harbor, he's stepping out onto the street and hailing a cab. He doesn't look like he's heading out to the clubs. He doesn't look like he's heading toward anything he'd enjoy at all. He ducks into the car like a doomed man.

Without thinking, I hail my own cab and tell the driver to follow.

We drive out of Honolulu and along the coast, our headlights sweeping along the dark and winding curves. As we go, we climb higher and higher along the cliffs, the sea rough and booming below us.

I don't know what I'm doing. My palms have gone clammy, which is impressive, given my kind barely have sweat glands. My driver keeps glancing in the rearview mirror at me.

Where are we going? What is Kaipo up to? What am I hoping to see?

Why am I invading his privacy like this?

I tell myself he's being secretive. I tell myself I need to know.

I need to know what kind of man is partnering with me, if I want to save my Reinhard.

Kaipo's taxi stops on the turn of a high headland, the red taillights pulsing on as Kaipo gets out. "Turn off your lights and wait back here," I tell my driver, and he does, pulling over on the steep grade leading up to the headland.

We sit in the dark and watch.

Kaipo hands his driver a tip and the red taillights turn off as the car slips away around the corner. Kaipo doesn't move right away. He's staring up at something across the road. After a moment, his shoulders rise in a big breath and he walks forward.

I pass my driver a crumple of bills. "Keep the change," I tell him.

I creep up the road, my bare feet noiseless on the asphalt. But for all the sharpness of my ears, I can't hear Kaipo ahead of me. All I can hear is the roar of the wind in the trees, the rustle of leaves and dropping of coconuts. The strident croaking of coqui frogs and the hum of crickets and katydids. It presses against my ears in a great, dreamy rumble.

When I round the bend, Kaipo is standing at the end of a driveway belonging to a house perched near the cliffs. The house is lit up with lights, and voices can be heard within, a commotion of life and happiness.

Kaipo seems to strain toward it, his barn door shoulders ridged up, his hands bunched. The shadows of the waving tree broughs dapple over him, and in that constant play of darkness and moonlight I make out an ache in his face I've never seen before. A twisted, wretched thing that trembles his lip up into a snarl, threatening to snap. And then he whirls, so suddenly I shrink back against the trunk of an ironwood tree. I wait there as Kaipo stalks across the road and out into the undergrowth on the cliffs, and I know this is it. This is my chance.

I sneak up to the driveway and peer at the mailbox glowing in the moonlight, and the name painted on its side.

It says KALAWAI'A.

My stomach doubles in weight.

The undergrowth on the cliff is thick and lush, overgrown. I fight through it, stumbling out onto rock to find Kaipo Kalawai'a standing at the cliff's edge.

My heart jumps into my throat.

He's pulled his shirt off, and the black geometry of his tattoos ripple in the moonlight. All his muscles clench in brutal definition as he fists his hands at his sides, and his howl of anguish is lost in the cracking boom of the sea below. Heat lightning flares far off in the dark, and it's as if he's calling it down. All the horrible weathers of the world and the heart. The waves crash. Seagulls ride the updrafts in wild rockings and wheelings of their wings, cawing brokenly. Kaipo tilts his head back, the thick bands of tendons standing in his neck as he screams, and an unexpected, stifled sob makes me suck my breath in.

Then Kaipo runs to the cliff's edge and dives.

My heart freefalls. I dash to the spot he'd been and look down.

Nothing but the raging sea, thundering against the cliffs in explosions of mist. It's swallowed him whole. He's killed himself.

The world distends.

Then—a head pops up on the frothing waves, shaking a black mane of hair out of its face, and I slump in relief. It's him. The powerful current sucks at him, tossing him about, and my back stiffens again. He's going to be dashed against the cliffs. He's going to drown.

I take a step back, ready to hurl myself off the cliff after him—

But he's stroking now. And he's a strong swimmer. He slices out of the sucking rollers and clambers onto a black coastal rock flooded with foam. He *is* a fisherman. A diver. He's going to be safe.

I don't know what I've witnessed. Something that feels mythic, dreamlike, like a dive into the spirit world. An angry rebirth. Something that holds the key to unlocking Kaipo Kalawai'a.

He stands on the rock and stares out at the embattled sea, shoulders heaving. Then he glances up at the cliffs.

I duck away and start hurrying back toward the road, my heart hushed within me. I don't want him knowing I've seen him in this moment. All I know now is that everything I thought I knew about Kaipo Kalawai'a was wrong.

# NINE

I don't know how to behave around Kaipo afterward.

When he gets back in the early hours of the morning, he's his old self. Happy-go-lucky, looking cleansed. No hint of the Kaipo I saw on that cliff. Nothing at all that would point toward a tormented past. Only his hair, still wet, proves that what I saw happened as he strides across the deck of the carrier ship.

I can't let it go. I have to pry.

"Out for a dive?" I call down to him.

He slows as he scales the ladder attached to the *Kanaloa*, then hops aboard. "Something like that."

He flashes me a grin and walks down the gangway, heading for below deck. His hand is on the sliding door to the bridge when I blurt it out.

"Why freediving?"

He pauses, broad shoulders suddenly tensed, head down in thought. "It's . . . peaceful." He glances at me, sees elaboration is in order and shrugs. "When you dive, you leave everything behind you. Even yourself." He squints out at the cliffs of Oahu, a strange look in his eyes. "Sometimes I need that."

A silence stretches, and he seems to come back to himself. He flashes me a grin, the old Kaipo again, and dips inside.

That's not enough for me. Not even close. As soon as we swap shifts and I shut the door to the master cabin behind me, I investigate.

There must be more to find about Kaipo.

Nothing on the nightstand besides Hemingway. Nothing in the top shelf of the closet besides some books on spearfishing and freediving and mental health.

It's in the bottom drawer of his closet that I find the shadow box.

It's a military display case with a wood frame and glass lid. Its black felt is pinned with ribbons, a Purple Heart and Navy Master Diving insignia with an old-fashioned diving mask with an open-circuit breathing apparatus. And there's a photo, too. It shows a group of friends posing in front of a naval ship, swim fins in hand and welding helmets in the crooks of their arms, Kaipo in the center looking almost unrecognizable with a buzzcut and a beardless, unsmiling face.

He looked so different then . . .

And he was a Navy diver. An underwater welder. He has all that experience and he let me poke fun at him and call him an amateur.

My cheeks bloom with a blush.

I'm an idiot. A stupid, callous idiot.

Something else glints in the faint light. There's another photo back there in the drawer. A photo of a family standing in front of the house on that cliff. Two young and pretty sisters standing in front of a freckle-faced, kindly-looking woman. And Kaipo, looking no older than eighteen, standing beside a craggy and grim-looking man who must be his father. Everyone has their arms around each other except Kaipo and his dad. Even though they stand almost shoulder to shoulder, the rift between them is clear. Kaipo keeps his arms tucked behind him, as if he can't bear touching the Kalawai'a patriarch, and so his father keeps his hands clasped in front of him, looking sullen and hurt.

The pain in the photo is undeniable.

I carefully place the photo and shadow box back where they were and ease the drawer shut, climb into bed and lie there with my eyes staring unseeingly up at the ceiling.

# TEN

After Hawaii, it's a straight shot to Hong Kong. Which means three weeks at sea. Three weeks without making port.

Too long to go without feeding.

I wait until I know Kaipo is asleep before I slip out of the *Kanaloa*. For some reason, I don't want him knowing what I'm doing.

I jump onto the neighboring boat without a sound. They haven't even locked their doors, as they've no need to out here. At least, they didn't think they did.

I flow like a shadow inside, through the galley and down the stairs where the cabins are. There's two of them—the mate and the engineer. From their breath, I know the mate is the drunker of the two, which means he's the least likely to wake.

I flow up onto his bunk and crouch over him like a nightmare. His chest rises and falls in his sleep, his lashes brushing against his cheek like a child's. He lies on his side, which means his neck arches back, baring the quiver of an artery there.

Saliva fills my mouth.

I place one hand on his head, the other on his shoulder, and dip my mouth to the meaty arch of his neck. My canines press—ever so gently—against skin, then pierce through, and warmth fills my mouth.

I drink the mate down.

Without quite knowing why, I start feeling guilty around Kaipo and avoid him even more than before. There are times when I wake, though, and he's not ready for sleep. I might find him doing crunches on the aft bridge deck, the failing light of sunset flaming his stomach into a rigid grid of abs. Or doing pull-ups from the rod holder arch on the fishing cockpit, the muscles of his back flaring into wings.

My gaze lingers for a moment. And then I tear it away with almost painful force.

I didn't respect him before. I can admit that. I've never trusted people who are both attractive and happy. As if they're cursed—or blessed—with a soft veil of stupidity that makes them immune to the hardships of life. I thought that somehow made me better than them—that I could live life more fully than them. But really, all it was, in the end, was ugly envy. That others could live in such sweet ignorance.

But now I know better. Now I know that Kaipo's carefree façade masks something deeper and darker.

That changes things.

We get closer with the *Kanaloa*. Kaipo finishes the main cabin floor, uses the extra teak to replace rotten boards out on deck. I get through the last of the replacement parts in the guest cabins, and Kaipo starts renovating them so I can move out of the master cabin. Slowly but surely, the items on our list get checked off.

And more and more—almost every night now—I slip out in the dark hours and feed.

Soon, there are whispers on the carrier. Men sharing stories of nightmares they've had. Nightmares of a pale woman haunting the ship. A shadow that came to them in the dead of night. A shadow with red eyes that drank their blood.

Eventually, Kaipo starts giving me strange looks, and I know he's heard the stories. But he spares me the humiliation of asking.

I've never felt so embarrassed of what I am before. Angry, yes. Oh, so angry. But never this feeling. It wrenches at me, leaving me flushed and heated and restless with agitation.

At last, our checklist is completed, and we come to our final day at sea.

That night, I wake to find Kaipo lying in bed beside me.

My spine goes rigid. Then I scramble back, eyes wide. For a moment, I can't comprehend what I'm seeing. He must have had an exhausting day and couldn't wait for me to wake before going to sleep.

The fool. He should have woken me. Doesn't he know that—

But my thoughts tangle as my gaze snares on his skin. He's not wearing a shirt. He must not wear one when he sleeps. Of course. His golden skin gleams with beads of sweat, and his chest rises and falls, causing all his muscles to ripple, the tight web of brawn around his torso to shift in the shadows of the master cabin.

His eyes roll beneath his lids. He's having a dream. He murmurs something, bringing my eyes to his lips. They're very full, slightly parted, and I can see the indentations where he bites them when he thinks. I can see a vein pulsing at the corner of his mouth. When he turns his head, the tendons in his neck strain, revealing the branch of arteries there, pumping blood in a strong, steady rhythm.

Life, life, life.

My pupils dilate. A great, annihilating hunger surges within me, and my body is drawn back as if by the pull of a dark star. His scent, the smell of his blood, sweeps over me, hot and unpleasant. His heartbeat punches in my ears, booming, impossibly fast. Impossible to resist.

It wouldn't take much. I could lean, just a little, and place my fangs to his neck. They'd all but melt into flesh. And then I could be sucking him, tasting him, so light he wouldn't even notice—

My eyes snap open to find my fangs pricked against his skin.

My heart drops. I scramble back, far enough this time I tumble out of bed, and then I'm up, gasping, chest heaving. No, no, no, no, no—

I stumble up the stairs, out onto the deck, onto the catwalk of the carrier ship, away.

I didn't do that. I will never do that. Why did I—I don't even think that way about—

I bump hard into a wall of flesh.

"Hey, what the—" it says.

It's a man. A rider from one of our neighboring boats, wrapped in a windbreaker against the chill. He's having a midnight smoke.

He squints at me. "Aren't you Kaipo's little passenger—"

He never finishes. I leap onto him, snarling with need, and bury my fangs in his throat. His eyes go wide as we go down on the catwalk, but a scream never gets out of his mouth. Because I've ripped out his windpipe and spat it out in a spray of blood. Then I'm sucking him down, feeding in the bubbling trough of his neck, making ferocious sounds of passion. But it's not the passion of that old rage toward Volok and everything I've lost, everything I've suffered. Or not only that. It's also the helpless whimper of something almost like erotic bliss as the man's eyes roll to the whites and his body twitches under me.

When I lift my head up to look at him, he's a corpse.

Horror fills me.

This can't be. I can't be caught doing this. I can't have Kaipo seeing me having done this.

I kick at the body and roll it off the catwalk.

Far below, I hear a splash. It's gone. I did it. I murdered someone.

I lie back on the catwalk, my hands balled in my hair. I croak out a sob. What did I do? Why did I do that? I've never done that. Not to an innocent. Why would I now—

But I know. The reason is sleeping back on the *Kanaloa*.

The reason is Kaipo.

I did it because I want him.

I did it because I'm attracted to him.

I shut my eyes, images of Reinhard crashing through my mind. No. No, I can't. Not that. I can't have that. I can't *do* that. I can't allow that to happen.

Guilt and shame scour my insides. I roll on the catwalk, holding my stomach, mouth open in a silent howl as tears stream out of my closed eyes.

Eventually, the guilt dissipates enough to leave me flat-backed and gasping on the catwalk. Then drawing in air in slow, calming inhalations. Then leaden with determination.

"What do you mean, I'm fired?"

Kaipo woke before dawn to find me sitting on the end of his bed—our bed—and I'd told him.

I'd told him what had to be done.

He shakes his head, trying to figure his way through it. "But I don't understand. We got the boat ready. I thought I'd shown you that I—"

"You did a great job on the boat," I interrupt. "It's not—it's not that. It's you."

"Me." He sounds as if he doesn't understand the word. "But what does that—"

"I can't tell you." What was there to tell, anyway? It's not like I feel anything for him. I know that. It's only a physical attraction. The smell of his blood. The temptation of his proximity.

It's not like he's anything special.

Right?

I sigh. "It doesn't matter. I just—I can't have you go with me. I'll just have to find someone else."

He looks down at his open hands as if expecting an answer there. The hurt in his face is like a dagger in my chest.

He shakes his head. "No. I'm meant to go with you. Arie sent you to me. She trusted *me* to do this, no one else. I'm not gonna have you hire some two-bit frogman you don't even know to—"

"I'll be all right—"

"*No!*" The forcefulness of the word shocks me silent. He cuts the edge of a palm down on the comforter. "You really expect to find another person with my experience on such short notice? You need someone with military experience. With diving experience. With boating experience. That is a very unique combination of skills." He glares up at me. "You want to find your husband?"

A lump bolts into my throat and I nod, my response almost a whisper. "Yes."

He jabs a finger into his chest. "Then I'm the best shot you have of getting him back. And you know it."

He's breathing hard when he finishes, his eyes on my face. I look away. He's right, I do know. The thought of botching my chance to find Reinhard now with the wrong help makes my chest clench. And the thought of turning Kaipo away when he looks like that—

I shut my eyes. "We can never sleep in the same bed again."

He sweeps his palms out to the side. "Done."

"And if I ever ask you to leave me, you do it."

He lifts a finger. "I won't abandon you without protection—"

"*Kaipo.*"

"Okay, done."

I slump my shoulders in a sigh. "Okay."

His brows draw up, his voice wavery with hope. "Okay?"

I draw in a long inhale, nod.

His face floods with relief. He nods back, as joyous as a little boy. "Okay."

And I sit there in the bed with him, feeling—I can't help it—my own sense of relief. Along with it the fear that I've made a grave mistake.

# ELEVEN

We arrive in Hong Kong within the hour.

It's still dark, the port buried in a thick haze of fog, its cranes and container terminals and high-suspension bridges looming like titans out of the gray wastes. As soon as we dock, the process of off-loading begins. I watch it all with my stomach in knots. The cargo bay floods with water. The divers go in again. The loadmaster paces the catwalks, barking into a VHF radio and ordering everyone to not start their engines or generators yet.

And I can't listen to any of it. Because I'm waiting for that rider's disappearance to be discovered.

I'm waiting to see how Kaipo will take it.

He stands beside me on the deck, bleary-eyed but eager to get going. He chats amiably with the divers in the water, helps the ship crew untie the *Kanaloa* from its mooring straps.

And as he does, a captain paces the deck of a yacht three boats away from us, his face white. "Billy?" He looks around in a panic. "Has anyone seen Billy?"

Kaipo glances his way, brow furrowed, and my heart leaps into my throat.

Then the loadmaster is barking into his radio again. "*Kanaloa*. Your turn."

And then we're drifting free from our cradle and floating off the boat, joining the other traffic in the harbor. The little wooden sampans sculling through the fog. The huge shapes of oil tankers and catamarans and hoverferries.

When I glance back, that captain is conferring with the loadmaster, lifting his arms in a gesture of mounting desperation.

I look at Kaipo on the flybridge.

But he's not looking. His eyes are ahead, focused on navigating us out of Hong Kong and toward our destination. He has no idea what happened.

Guilty relief leaks into me, and then I wonder why. Do I really care about what he thinks?

I do, I realize with a sinking in my gut. I really do.

I watch the back of Kaipo's magnificent head at the wheel and feel a creeping unease take hold of me. I haven't cared about what anyone has thought of me in a long time. I haven't, in fact, cared much about anything at all since Reinhard was taken from me and I was enslaved on Transmarinia. Besides my grief over Reinhard—which I eventually tempered into a constant, nagging loss that was always there but was no longer debilitating, no longer had the power to destroy—I cared about only one thing. The one thing that drove me. That kept me going, kept me clinging to life.

But now, a crack has appeared. Now, something new and unsettling. I don't like what that means.

I tell myself I can will it away, like I did with everything else. That can happen.

I leave Kaipo on the bridge without saying a word.

It takes us only a couple of hours to reach the coordinates of Castle Volok.

After the refit, the *Kanaloa* handles beautifully, a far cry from before. Kaipo is extremely pleased. He rubs the nav console as if it were a dog's coat and hisses through clenched-together teeth, "That's my girl." His mood only fades when we arrive at the spot on the South China Sea where the ruin of the castle is supposed to lie. He kills the engines and puts the *Kanaloa* into stabilizing mode, and we both go to the gunwale and peer over the side.

Under the ripple of the waves, it slowly materializes, vague and wavy: a steep black pyramid of a castle, its two towers sunken and leaning, tunneling down into the gloom. All of it giving off a faint green emanation as of the gases of something decomposing.

The little hairs on my nape rise.

"So that's her," Kaipo says.

I swallow. "That's her."

"Charming." Kaipo lifts a pair of binoculars. "Better make sure we don't have any friends nearby." He shimmies up the ladder to the tuna tower and glasses the horizon. I don't follow him, choosing instead to wait in the shade of the open fishing cockpit. I don't need binoculars. My unnaturally sharp eyes already give me the answer before Kaipo hops back down.

"Not a yacht in sight. We're alone out here." He leans over the gunwale again to assess the vague shape of those ruins in the deep. "So where's this atlas?"

"In the castle archives. In a steel safe. But I don't know the combination."

He nods to himself. "So we'll have to cut it open." He peels his shirt over his head and tosses it aside, sits down on a bench and pulls a caddy filled with diving gear toward him.

I place my hands on my hips. "What are you doing?"

He looks at me as if he's concerned I'm slow. "I'm the diver . . .?"

Not so fast, Herr Kalawai'a. "No. I'm the one diving."

He pauses, one hand on the rubbery folds of a wetsuit. "What?" He snorts, shaking the idea off. "No, you're not. You haven't dived before."

"Then you can teach me."

He lets out a sharp laugh. "I think you're forgetting that underwater cutting is *extremely* dangerous—"

"And as the Shipwright of Transmarinia, you know I have plenty of cutting experience."

He stops to blink at me now. "You're serious."

I cross my arms over my chest. I am.

He lets go of the wetsuit and stands, reaches up to grab the fishing arch so he can squint at me, hip cocked. "And *when* exactly were you going to tell me this? I'm the one trained for underwater salvaging—"

"And I'm the one who knows the castle."

His brows pinch into a furrow. "How?"

I shift my weight, feeling suddenly self-conscious. "Because I built it."

His stare is unreadable. A narrowing of the eyes, as if he's working through his feelings about this, or why I won't back down. His voice is low with wonder. "They really did enslave you, didn't they?"

I feel my cheeks grow hot, but I won't look away. Nor will I tell him that, somehow, diving down there and plundering the archives will feel like facing something. Will feel like penance.

For what I did. For helping Volok.

For the irrational but unavoidable feeling that I've somehow let Reinhard down all these years.

Maybe he sees all that in my eyes, though. Because he pinches his nose and blows out a breath in a resigned way. "This is crazy."

"I hired you," I remind him. "And this is an order. Someone needs to stay topside to keep a lookout for the Sons of Volok." I take the swimsuit from him and look it over, look back up into his face. "So, Herr Kalawai'a. Teach me how to dive."

# TWELVE

"You following me so far?"

Kaipo's checking the fit of my heavy-duty underwater diving suit as I stand in the fishing cockpit, feeling like an astronaut, my head swirling with the diving basics he's just gone through. I dip my chin in a dazed nod.

"Okay." He hefts a cylindrical steel air tank filled to 3000 psi, wipes a thumb across the Braille scripture of its manufacturer, serial number and test date. "As . . . well, as the undead, you don't need to breathe, obviously."

I think of lying in that claustrophobic bower of coral under the sea, and my gut tightens.

He lugs the air tank to a BCD or buoyancy compensating device, a thick black vest sprouting a tentacular dangling of hoses. He buckles the tank into it with two black straps tightened with cams, connects the inflator to the BCD and depresses it with his thumb until the bladders of the vest inflate in an unwrinkling of black nylon. "But you'll need air to communicate with me up top." He hefts a comm rope. A hardwire underwater communication system with comm wires built into its core.

I grimace as he connects the rope to the bulky diving helmet I'll be using. "Can't we do wireless communication?"

He shakes his head as he uses his teeth to rip off a length of electrical insulating tape, wraps it around the comm rope connection to waterproof it. "This is more reliable. I don't want you cutting out on me down there. You're already gonna have to be lugging around the other hoses anyway."

The other hoses. The grounding cable to safeguard against electrocution. And O2 and electrical lines feeding from a fuel tank and welding generator into an oxyarc cutting torch.

I lift the torch and inspect it. It looks like a garden hose with a hollow rod stuck into its holder like the beak of some bizarre bird. It feels capable. Dangerous.

Kaipo glances at it as he finishes insulating the helmet. "I know you cut and weld. You done it underwater, though?"

My attempt to shrug fails under the weight of everything on me. "I'll manage."

"It's a whole other beast, honey. The electrode"—he taps the tip of the torch—"it uses an oxygen jet to split the water molecules into oxygen and hydrogen atoms. Which can—"

"Go boom."

He fires a finger-gun at me: Bingo. "So don't dillydally. Get in and get out, and start high and cut downward. You don't want gas to get trapped in your cutting space with you and form pockets. If you hear any popping noises, that's your sign to get out of dodge."

I nod. "Got it."

He tucks the torch rod into my fine-grade mesh diving bag, clips the bag onto the BCD and helps me shoulder the whole thing. I nearly buckle from the weight.

He circles me for a final check, and his big callused hands seem to be everywhere as he clicks in dog-collar snaps and cinches up straps and cummerbunds. He velcros my waist strap so snug I feel a strange thrill in my stomach I'm not sure has anything to do with the harness, and when he snaps my chest strap in place it pushes my breasts together under the diving suit and the thought of those rough hands on my body flashes through my mind.

My chest and face grow hot. What am I thinking?

"We don't know what else could be flammable down there," he's saying. "Methane. Hydrocarbon. Carbon monoxide. So make your cuts as quick as possible." He steps back to take me in, his lips on the verge of a pout. "You really should have another diver with you."

For a moment, I waver. Much to my surprise, I want him to come, too.

I don't know what's come over me.

I always do things alone. It's all I've ever known since Reinhard left. And I need to face this by myself.

"Too bad we need one of us to stay topside to give me power." I point at the huge 24V DC battery with its "on" and "off" switch my electrical cable is snaked into. "Plus, you need to watch out for those cultists, remember?"

He looks as if he wants to say something, but he bites it back, picks up the helmet. "Ready?"

I nod, and he lowers the twenty-pound monstrosity over my head, clicks it into place. The sudden seal is like a noose around my neck. My breathing sounds loud in my ears. Most of the day's glare is blessedly blocked out, but the oppressive closeness of everything is suffocating, and for a moment I'm under the sea again, perpetually drowning—

"Hey." Kaipo grips my shoulders, his voice muffled through the helmet. "You okay?"

I nod, the helmet like a millstone around my neck, my breath shallow in my lungs. Kaipo looks dubious but flicks on a dive radio and puts on a headset, his voice suddenly pouring into my small world. "Can you hear me?"

"Yeah," I manage, pushing down a furious surge of embarrassment.

But he doesn't joke, doesn't take the opportunity to say this is a bad idea. He gives me a thumbs up. "Let's get you in the water, then."

He walks me over to the starboard side where he opens a door in the gunwale for access to the water. A steel ladder there hooked onto the boat. The chop dips and swells, and a sudden nausea rolls through me. I fix my eyes on that blurry shape below.

Down there, I'll find my answers. Down there, I'll get closer to Reinhard.

I have to rotate my whole body to look at Kaipo. He's watching me closely, looking unhappy. He lifts his hands to grip my helmet. "You got this. Okay?" He taps his headset. "I'll be right with you."

I nod, almost bashing my forehead on the faceplate of my helmet.

"And if I tell you those Sons of Volok bastards are coming, you get your ass topside. No messing around. You understand?"

*He's worried*, I realize. *He's worried about me*. His concern changes something in me, brings on a clarifying calm. I nod again.

"Okay." He steps back, mollified. His Adam's apple dips in a swallow. "Good luck."

And without waiting for any other doubts to present themselves, I jump off the *Kanaloa* into the water.

# THIRTEEN

Dropping down into the sun-shot cold, the thick multi-colored braid of my cables trailing after me like a strange umbilical cord. A whirl of bubbles around me. I keep my thumb on the dump valve by my shoulder, venting air from my BCD until I've descended two meters below the surface. It gets dark almost instantly, the beams of light from the upper world fading away.

"Ilsa? You there?" Kaipo's voice crackles in my earphones, slightly muffled.

Despite myself, I feel a rush of comfort. "I'm here."

"What's it like up close?"

I look down, and then I see what's cohering below me, filling up my faceplate like a baroque vision.

My eyes can't get big enough.

"Yeah," I gulp. "It's something."

I turn on my divelight and play it over Castle Volok, my breath stilling in my lungs.

Whatever the Redfearns did to sink it, they did a bang-up job. Its sheets of black glass have been blasted out, leaving gaping holes for the entry of fish. Its pylons have been crumpled and crushed, leaving the whole edifice to sink to the seafloor at a precarious angle. But still. There is a dignity to it yet. A hunger. Its broken drawbridge yawns like a black mouth. Green algae glows on its walls, pulsing like a siren's call. Forests of seaweed sway about it like the hair of drowned women, hiding the toothsome rusticles mantling its base.

It waits. And it hungers.

There's a sharp cold in my head, like my ears need to pop. I'm cold all over.

I've never seen it before. Never been allowed to lay eyes on my work.

It's both beautiful and terrible.

I lazily kick my fins, using my breath like Kaipo taught me to adjust my buoyancy and drop lower. I trail a hand along a sleek tower, scraping up a slick green biofilm. I can remember drawing up the blueprints for this place. Sketching out its lines, its chambers for those I knew would be brought there to suffer. Who would die screaming.

I shut my eyes and concentrate. The archives. The left tower. Third floor from the top.

I thank the Redfearns for their pyrotechnics and glide through the shattered window and inside the castle.

The beam of my divelight roams across a place taken over by the deep. Leaning marble shelves veined with phosphor are now coated in a bristling growth of sponges and anemones and dead man's fingers. Small fish dart in and out of the light. And tube worms, like wriggling masses of maggots, gorge on the books everywhere in the room.

But I only have eyes for the tall portrait hung on the wall.

It once depicted a noble. Turkish, perhaps. Fiercely browed. Romantically caped. Wearing a fur hat with a brooch and plume. But there's nothing much left of him. Great patches of paint have smeared or flaked off, and dark blooms of what looks like mold or algae have migrated across a canvas torn at the edges by a swollen and warped wooden frame.

There's no knowing if they built the archives the way I designed it. There's no knowing if this is the right painting.

Only one way to find out.

I lift the portrait off the wall and set it aside, its shadow slipping away to reveal a hulking box of black steel with a combination lock. It must weigh half a ton.

I whistle. "I found the safe."

Kaipo sighs in my ear. "Good. The sooner you're out of there, the better."

I open my diving bag, take out the torch rod and fit it into the torch. Then I flip down the little welding shield lens mounted onto my helmet and the top half of my vision tints dark. "Okay. Make me hot."

There's a pause, then a naughty grin in Kaipo's voice. "Don't you mean make *it* hot?"

"Right," I mumble, feeling my cheeks warm. "That."

I can almost see him shaking his magnificent head. "Knife switch hot."

I wait a moment for the oxygen to travel from the tank on the *Kanaloa* above and down through the oxygen cable into the torch. And I wait. There's a rumbling, bubbling sound. I press the torch rod against the safe and pull the trigger. There's a stream of bubbles, and then a sparking ball of fire erupts into being, making the torch rod look like a wand casting a spell. Only the arc shine isn't orange; it's as green as witchfire in the welding lens. An uncanny, wavering emerald glow that looks like ectoplasm. A blast of sorcery. Muscling the rod hard against the safe, I gouge a long kerf into the steel over the top of the combination lock. Heated slag falls away, turning molten orange as it drops below the shade of my welding lens. It looks like globs of magma.

"Ilsa?" Kaipo asks.

"Kinda busy here," I grunt.

"There's a boat coming."

I release the trigger on the torch and the ball of fire disappears. "And?"

"It's too far to be certain yet. But the flag—it could be the Sons of Volok."

I curse under my breath.

"It'll be here within the next fifteen minutes. We need to get you out of the water. Now."

But I shake my head, a clumsy swishing back and forth of my helmet. "No." I turn the torch back on and resume cutting. "I'm almost there. I'm not leaving without that atlas."

"Mother—" But his curse dies on his lips as a series of muffled pops go off in the archives. His voice goes flat. "What was that?"

I stiffen, remembering his warning. *Fuck.* "Nothing."

"Don't you fuck with me. I heard that. The oxygen hydrogen mixtures are forming gas pockets above you, aren't they?"

I don't need to look up. I can see it now, a vast colony of silvery gas pockets wobbling on the ceiling of the archives like some liquid nightmare, waiting for one stray spark to ignite it into a glory of devouring flame.

"You need to stop now and get your ass out of there."

"I. Told. You," I grit through clenched teeth, making my last cut. Steam billows upward toward the ceiling, carrying with it stray sparks of light, and I curse.

"Fuck, this was a bad idea," Kaipo groans. His voice goes in and out, as if he's pacing the deck. Then he falls silent. He's made a decision. "I'm coming down there—"

"No, you're not."

"Ilsa!"

But with a burst of bubbles, my cut is complete. The square burns orange around the lock, its jagged edges of metal glowing. I flip up my welder's lens, grab the handle to the safe door and pull hard. One of the cuts apparently wasn't deep enough at one of the corners; the block of metal twists partly open, but it's enough for me to peer inside with my divelight.

There's only a single item inside: a long black plastic cylinder.

"There's something in here. It might be the atlas."

"Well hurry up and grab it. We need to go."

"Just one more pass." I pull the trigger on the torch, and there's a burst of bubbles—then nothing.

I frown. "Did you turn off the oxygen?"

"What?" Kaipo sounds distracted. Probably looking through binoculars. "No. Why?"

Doesn't matter. I take out a pair of bolt cutters, bash them hard against the pried-out block of metal until it's twisted out of the way. Then I reach in and manually pull the lock mechanism inward, swing the safe open.

I can see what that plastic cylinder is now: a watertight drafting tube. A container used for architectural drawings, engineering blueprints, posters, artwork. And maps.

A container for Volok's atlas.

I grin, flushed with triumph. "Found it."

"Seriously?" Kaipo lets out a low whoosh of air. I can practically see him closing his eyes in relief. "Okay, get topside. Now. The boat's seen us—"

His voice cuts out in a sharp burst of static, and my gut clenches.

"Kaipo?" I feel my helmet for the comm rope. Still connected.

Something cold lodges against my sternum. I don't want to, but I turn about in the water. My revolving body pulls on the braid of cables sprouting from my suit, and their ends float inside the window into the archives. They've been cut. All of them. The grounding cable. The comm rope. The electrical lead. The severed oxygen cable trailing a stream of bubbles.

And that's when I see the shapes drifting past the other paneless windows of the archives, heading toward the windowframe nearest me. They look like a school of ghosts or terrible angels. Their hair rippling in the water. Their skin as pale as moonlight. Their executive suits evoke drowned and undead CEOs.

My pulse knocks in my ears. My flesh crawls. I feel like an idiot.

The danger was never from topside. The Sons of Volok were down here the whole time.

# FOURTEEN

My lungs seize, and I forget how to breathe.

I don't think. In a burst of kicks, I fly down one of the aisles in the maze of bookshelves, scuba fins undulating behind me. I max out my speed by groping along the shelves with my hands and pulling myself along, sending books and sea urchins tumbling in my wake. I'm still holding the bolt cutters, and I whirl around to look behind me, ready to use them like a bat.

But there's nothing. I'm alone in a T-section in the shelves, my breathing loud and strained in my ears. My brain a boiling clot of terror. What am I going to do? I can't signal to Kaipo for help. And I'm trapped down here. I'm trapped and they're going to find me and then they're going to find Kaipo and—

A hard tug sucks me backward, and I shriek and spin to find pallid hands gripping my severed cables, pulling me toward a mouth jammed with teeth as sharp as a barracuda's. My response is pure instinct: I jab down with the bolt cutters and clip the cables. The sudden release sends the cultist tumbling away and I kick my fins, eeling around a corner—

Only to bump into another Son of Volok.

Fangs snap at me, trying to pierce through the thick fabric of my suit. The thing's pale flesh looks curdled, almost rotting, like damp cheese. Here and there embedded with clusters of small barnacles. They must always stay down here, guarding the sunken castle of their old Commodore.

It must have driven them half mad.

The guardian swipes at my helmet with a clawed hand, the blunt force of the blow dazing me and sending cracks spiderwebbing across the faceplate. It lifts its hand again, and this time I manage to raise my bolt cutters between us and catch a descending finger between the blades.

The bolt cutters clip the finger in two as neatly as a candle.

Blood billows into the water in inky crimson skeins and the Son of Volok snarls, fangs snapping as it clutches its hand. Then it's pinned my wrists back against a shelf. My air tank clunks behind me. Marine growth digs into my back. Then the cultist is pressing its brow to my faceplate. Its mouth swells as a wide as a shark's, promising vengeance.

It rears that head back and butts it against the faceplate.

The spidery cracks leap and spread.

Again. More cracks. The sound like ice about to shatter.

Oh, no.

The next butt does it. Glass gives way and water rushes in. It engulfs my helmet, pours down my throat, filling up my lungs and closing off my scream. For a moment, I am lost in memories of drowning, of sleeping below the sea. Death and undeath.

Then the cultist and I are staring at each other, shards of glass floating in winks of light between us.

It ungapes its jaws.

My skin contracts all over my body.

But those jaws never close. Suddenly, something sharp and deadly-looking has punched out of them. Barbed, silvery. The tip of a spear. The cultist's eyes widen, trying to make sense of what has happened. Then those eyes break up with capillaries and blood begins to float in a red cloud around that grisly head.

The spear sucks out of that stoven skull and the corpse is pushed aside. Through a dizzying rush of relief, I find myself staring into Kaipo's deep-brown eyes.

He came for me. He didn't even bother with putting on a diving suit. Or even a respirator.

He's freediving.

His hands feel my face, my suit, checking for signs of injury. I shake my head, give him a thumbs up.

He nods, his mane of hair flowing in an eddy of rich brown around him. He looks like a sea god. He holds a Hawaiian sling—a sort of bow with rubber tubing attached to the spear so he can reuse it. He readies it and waves a hand to me: *Follow*.

I unclip the straps to my air tank and slither out of them, unscrew my heavy helmet and let it float away. Then I follow.

We meet another Son of Volok coming out of the bookshelves, and Kaipo doesn't hesitate. He raises the sling and sticks the cultist in the forehead as neatly as skewering a grouper. Its eyes roll up and he tugs the spear free and points to the window we came in.

He starts to kick off, but I grab his arm and point at the safe.

He shakes his head and grabs my shoulder, points past me.

A horde of cultists are floating out of the archive's library like a shoal of the undead. Slug-white and grinning, eyes like pale eggs. There must be fifty of them. Maybe more.

They keep coming.

But I can't. Reinhard's face pops into my head, and I know. I can't leave. Not without the atlas.

I kick away toward the safe.

Kaipo's teeth grit and he grabs for me, but I slip out of reach. He shakes his head, bubbles streaming from his mouth in a restrained curse, and he twists about and pulls back on his sling, spearing the closest cultist through the heart.

We don't have much time.

I dart a hand into the broken safe and snatch the drafting tube's shoulder strap, kick away again.

Kaipo is swimming backward, trying to tug his spear free from the chest of an impaled cultist. I grab his arm and pull. *Time to go.*

He gives up, releasing the Hawaiian sling as he casts a look behind us.

The wave of vampires is rushing toward us in the silent gloom of the castle. Seconds behind.

The blood pulses in my skull.

Kaipo and I kick madly for the window. It's not far. The gas pockets have collected on the ceiling above it. Shiny, mercurial, jostling like eggs in the disturbed water.

This place is a deathtrap.

We float out of the window and with shaking hands I drop the weights on my diving belt, purge air from my tank into my BCD. The bladders of the vest fill with air and I start to ascend, Kaipo kicking upward at my side.

Not fast enough.

I look down, and past our flippers is a sight that belongs in a nightmare. The Sons of Volok are swarming out of the castle after us in plague of pale and rotting flesh as if a graveyard had been disinterred, the sea had given up its dead. All I can see is glowing eyes, mouths ringed with fangs like flukeworms, talons reaching up at us.

Kaipo and I lock eyes. The *Kanaloa* is still too far away, a shadow twenty feet above us. We're not going to make it.

So I do the only thing I can think of.

I pull a marine red signal flare out of my diving bag, remove the top and ignite the flare with the striker so its bubble of burning magnesium lights our faces in its furious glare.

Kaipo and I lock eyes. And I drop it.

We don't wait. We kick up again, arms propelling madly, trying to put as much distance between us as we can. I don't know what the chances are of it even working. I glance down, catch the flare drop into that swarm of the undead, its red, sulfurous light dropping down, down, down toward that window of the archives. And the gas pockets there.

And then it's gone, swallowed up by the horde on our heels.

I've missed, I think. We're done for.

Those talons reach up, swiping at our fins. They're feet away now. This is the end.

I meet Kaipo's eyes. He's already looking at me, and I wonder what would have happened if I had known him longer. I wonder if we would have grown to care for each other. I wonder if I would have loved him.

Such a strange thought, here at the end of all things.

And then the world ends.

The sound of the explosion is a rumbling tidal wave through the water. It slams against my eardrums like the collision of tectonic plates, almost blacking me out. And then we see the flames below us. They mushroom upward in great bloomings of orange beauty like an evil lotus, unmaking the castle in stunning eruptions of steel and stone. And it does not stop. It comes on, rumbling up toward us, devouring that swarm of the undead as they shriek in agony, licking all the way up until those grasping at our flippers are engulfed in incandescent fire.

The concussion flings us upward in a tumbling of bubbles, and I shut my eyes and cling to Kaipo, the only safe place in this world, as everything scalds and burns around us. Here. Here is safe. Here is certainty.

And then, at last, the spinning stops. The world stills. And everything is all right.

I'm alive. With Kaipo. With a man who risked his life to come back and save me. And there's nothing more I want in this moment than to share what I'm feeling with him.

And when I look into his eyes, my grin that's stretching from ear to ear fades.

Because Kaipo is looking at me with wide eyes. His face is blotched white and blue, and he's convulsing, his stomach sucking in and out.

*No.*

The lack of oxygen is affecting his brain. We've been down here too long. We're ascending too fast for his body to handle it. He's about to go into a hypoxic blackout.

He's . . . drowning.

*No, no, no, no, no.*

I grab his arm and kick hard upward. We're only feet away. The surface is dancing above us, tantalizingly close.

*Hang on, Kaipo. Not now. Not after all that. Not when we're almost there—*

But Kaipo's kicking slows, the spasms overtaking him. I kick harder, teeth clenched, eyes burning in denial.

*No!*

But Kaipo bends over now in a series of uncontrollable spasms, all attempts at swimming gone. His ribcage clenches. He flings his head back, tendons standings in his neck, his shaggy surfer hair floating about him.

Then his eyes roll to the whites as he goes limp, and I grab him, my mouth opening to release my anguish in a torrent of bubbles.

*Noooooooooooooo!*

# FIFTEEN

I drag him onto the deck of the *Kanaloa*'s fishing cockpit and lay his head back to open his airway. He's not moving. His face has turned a ghastly shade of gray. I place an ear to his chest and listen, but I cannot hear it. His heart has stopped beating.

It's my fault. It's all my fault. If I'd gone topside when he asked, he wouldn't have come down for me. If I'd not stayed behind to grab the atlas, maybe he would have made it to the surface. Maybe he would be okay.

But I didn't. I did none of those things. I was greedy. I couldn't let go of my anger. My need for vengeance.

I killed him.

My eyes burn. I let out a wrenching sound that's part sob, part snarl of anger and grab the AED kit from the diving caddy, drag it to Kaipo's side. No. I can still save him. I have to.

I have to.

I stick the pads to his skin and try to plug the cables into the AED. My hands are shaking so badly I can't get the connectors in, the brass ends scraping uselessly around the holes. "Fuck!" I shout and almost smash the AED into pieces on the deck. I curl my fingers into fists and shut my eyes a moment, breathe in hard through my nose, then try again. Finally, they slip in, and the relief is a blast of hope in my lungs. I push the charge button and wait, rocking on my heels, hissing through gritted teeth. "Come on, come on . . ."

At last, it blinks to full charge.

I punch the shock button.

Kaipo arches up and slaps back onto the deck, as limp and lolling as a boned fish. I cock my ear to listen.

Nothing.

A rising despair pushes against the back of my throat. I interlace my fingers and start doing compressions. I make the mistake of glancing over the gunwale and see the distant shape of a yacht approaching, a black flag fluttering from its bow. It has a green V on it.

My jaw clenches.

I swipe tendrils of wet surfer hair off Kaipo's face, pinch his nose and place my mouth around his, blow hard to fill his lungs. Then back to compressions. "You can't leave now," I scold him. "You promised you'd help me, remember? You said you'd find my Reinhard." I blow into his mouth again, start another round of compressions, my voice starting to get away from me. "We're not done. I still need you, asshole." I hiccup a sob and pound on his chest with a fist, screaming. "Wake up, goddamn it! *Wake up!*"

And he does.

His deep brown eyes snap open and he coughs up a spew of water, rolls onto his side to puke up what looks like half the ocean. My heart drops. The relief is staggering, leaving me lightheaded and wanting to laugh. I could almost puke with him. And then Kaipo is blinking at me, eyes wide in astonishment, as if the heavens had opened. "You didn't leave me," he croaks, a break in his voice that puts a twinge in my heart. "You . . . you fought for me . . ."

Something close to embarrassment coils in my gut. I open my mouth, but I don't know what to say.

Then he's crushing me in a hug, his muscly arms wrapping around me to dwarf my body with his own. He's clinging onto me as if I am the only still point in this world. "Thank you," he breathes into my ear.

For a moment, I kneel there, rigid. Then I tentatively put my arms around him. This isn't just a reaction to nearly dying. This is a trauma response. There's something deeper behind this. It blocks up my throat.

As back on those cliffs in Honolulu, I feel as if I am witnessing something I shouldn't. A ferocious vulnerability. It brings up in me a great tenderness, a softening that leaves my heart bruised and aching. And in those arms, I feel—I can't help it—like I'm home.

Guilt shivers through me. I know I shouldn't be feeling this way. I know that, if I had lost him, I would have fallen. I've tried to convince myself that I was only relieved because I need him. That in my mind I've assigned him a practical purpose, as with all my other relationships over the past few centuries, so I can hold onto my anger.

But I know better. This relief—this harrowing, throat-narrowing, chest-numbing relief—betrays what's in my heart. And I can no longer lie to myself.

It's not just a physical attraction. It's not only that I want to drink his blood.

I care for him.

I close my eyes. This isn't good. I need to find Reinhard. Soon.

When I open my eyes and look over Kaipo's shoulder, I see the Sons of Volok boat.

My spine stiffens.

"Come on," I tell Kaipo, gently disengaging from that wonderful, terrible embrace. "We have to go."

He nods and wipes at his eyes, allows me to help him to his feet and follows me to the bridge.

When we speed away across the waves, I look back. But we're not being followed. The Sons of Volok boat has stopped over the site of Castle Volok, and pale-skinned men in sharp suits are diving into the water. As if looking for something.

I look at the drafting tube in my hand.

When we're sure no one's following us, and there's no longer any flash of steel or glass or fiberglass on the horizon, we put the *Kanaloa* into stationary mode and inspect the atlas.

Kaipo sits on a bench at the chart table. He looks better. Less pale. The color returned to his cheeks.

I've wrapped a blanket around his massive shoulders and he sips from a water bottle I've given him, looking a little rueful, as if he's not used to feeling weak. Or embarrassed.

But he leans forward in curiosity as I unscrew the top of the drafting tube and slide out the atlas.

It's heavy, bound in black leather like an occult codex, a sorcerer's grimoire. Its cover has faded gilt lettering: ATLAS NOSFERATUS. It crackles when I open it. The parchment is very old, age toned. There's an oval world map near the front. It's titled MAPPA NOSFERATUS MUNDUS.

"A map of the Lairverse," Kaipo intones, awe in his voice.

That's what this atlas is. Charts for all the landmarks in this nautical world of the undead.

My hands are shaking as I turn the pages.

One chart after another. Islands and atolls and coastlines, all painstakingly depicted in fantastically colored drawings. Some of them dating back centuries to the early days when vampires first took to the sea, the style ornate and decorated with sailing ships and floating coffins and winged shadows. Others look more recent, the sketches simpler and less faded. Each folio crosshatched with meridian lines and titled in an elegant hand: SANGUISUGA, HIBERNACULA, BLOODTOWN, THE GRAVEYARD OF LAIRS.

I start to speed up as I go, the adrenaline kicking in, and the places whip by, faster and faster. The pages beginning to blur.

And then my hand freezes, the corner of a page pinched between two fingers.

THE HOLE OF SOULS.

I let the page fall, and we both lean in.

It's a chart depicting the strait of water between Asia and Africa, with a graphic scale and rhumb lines radiating from the points of a compass rose. But it's the inset card that draws attention. A blown-up part of the chart in the lower righthand corner. A sketch of a coastal mangrove swamp called *The Bay of the Dead*. In the heart of the maze of waterways in that swamp, a blue hole. The center of the hole is done in blackest ink, as if it were a doorway to some nether realm. A warning in Latin under it: *HIC SVNT STRIGAE*.

*Here lie vampires.*

A chill creeps down my spine.

"*Mare Rubrum*," Kaipo reads, bringing my attention back up to the strait of water between the two continents.

I nod. "The Red Sea." And I look at the dot circled in that water, and the name of the country beside it.

I meet Kaipo's gaze. "We're going to Egypt."

# SIXTEEN

We leave straightaway.

I go below to get some sleep. The daylight is giving me a throbbing headache, and I'm beyond exhausted. Kaipo insists he'll be fine on his own, and I tell him to wake me if he spots the Sons of Volok.

When I shut myself in the master suite, I'm afraid I'll be overtaken by a churning of conflicted feelings that will leave me stranded on the sheets for hours, tossing and turning. But I fall asleep as soon as my head hits the pillow.

I dream of Reinhard.

Water rushes down my lungs, suffocating me. But it's not water. It's hair, black and diseased. Rat hair. Squirming bodies are in my mouth, sharp nails scrabbling, slicing my gums open and clicking against my teeth, trying to burrow down my throat.

I wake gasping and clutching my neck, chest heaving, a scream on my lips.

It's dark. I was sleeping. Only a dream.

I cover my eyes with a hand and lean down against the sheets.

When I've shaken off the last vestiges of that dream, I go abovedeck to find we're at anchor on the sea. Where, I don't know. There's a glittering of lights far off on our starboard side. The coastline of some island or country.

Of Kaipo, though, there is no sign. He's not in the bridge, or in his fighting chair in the fishing cockpit.

I know where he'll be.

I climb up the aft ladder to find him in the tuna tower, seated at the helm with a pair of binoculars in his lap. He looks relaxed but bone-tired, dark rims under his eyes. He squints up at me. "Hey."

"Hey." I sit beside him and we listen to the water lapping against the hull. There's not a soul anywhere to be seen.

"No sign of anyone following us?"

He shakes his head.

I study him. "How are you?"

He scrunches one eye shut and scratches his neck. "Embarrassed?"

I snort. "No offense, but diving sucks."

"Hey now." He laughs. "Don't knock it until you've tried freediving, baby."

"Uh-huh." I watch him as he turns the binoculars over in his hands, the panes catching the starlight. "Thank you, by the way."

He looks at me.

"For diving down for me. You saved my life."

"And you mine." He shifts in his seat, and I know he's thinking about his reaction after I revived him. He opens his mouth to say something.

"You don't have to explain," I tell him, softly.

"I want to, though." His hands have begun to shake, and he sets the binoculars aside on the helm station, rubs his palms together to still them. "My parents, they were . . . different. They homeschooled me and my sisters, raised us in a house shut off from everyone."

I think of that mailbox stamped with KALAWAI'A on Honolulu.

"It wouldn't be until I was older that I'd realize they were mentally unwell. When my mom met my dad, she told him she'd had a vision of having a family with him. They broke up their marriages, ran off to another island in Hawaii to raise us. They had . . . very specific plans for us. And so they were very hard on us. I was the only one in the family to recognize it as abuse. My sisters, they were too enmeshed in their trauma bond with my parents to see it. But I grew to resent my father."

That photo. A teenaged Kaipo barely touching his father.

"One night, my father was chewing me out as he always did. Calling me terrible things. Telling me no one was ever going to love me. And . . . I couldn't take it anymore." He draws a trembling hand down his face. "And I screamed at him. Told him to get the fuck away from me. I was twenty-three. I'd never done anything like that before. I'd never shouted at him before. It terrified my dad. Showed him I wasn't afraid of him anymore. That I was willing to stand up to him."

His breathing is starting to get fast and uneven, and I don't think about it. I reach out and take his hand.

He grips it hard.

"I'd moved out by then, but I was still very close with my family. So I was shocked when I was ostracized from the holidays. My father was claiming that I was violent. That he was afraid I was going to assault him. He was claiming that my—that my fiancée at the time was abusing me and getting between me and the family. I kept hearing all these awful rumors, things my dad had made up to turn everyone against me. Soon my sisters stopped calling and avoided me, not wanting any part of it. They'd believed the smear campaign. I was furious. I wanted to defend my fiancée and make the family a safe place for her, confront my dad about his behavior, and my dad knew that. So he refused to give me the opportunity. He wasn't going to allow me to be a part of the family again until I stopped holding him accountable for what he did. And he did that by giving me the silent treatment for a year as a form of punishment and control. Left me to stew in that anger. And . . . it destroyed me." He shuts his eyes, remembering. "It was like being boiled alive in a cauldron of shame. His silence told me that not only did my feelings not matter, but that *I* didn't matter. That I was worthless, and unworthy of love. And when I could no longer love myself . . ." His breath hitches, and he bites the inside of his lip to steady himself. "That meant

I couldn't love my fiancée anymore, either. I couldn't be there for her. All the time, I was stuck in my thoughts, replaying the trauma over and over. I became irritable. I couldn't be present. I couldn't be the partner she needed. So she left me. And only then did my father allow me back into the family." He lets out a strange, twisted laugh. "Only it wasn't a family anymore. Because the illusion had been lifted, and I finally realized that I'd never had a family."

I let out a long, stunned breath I didn't know I was holding. "Wow." I feel numb, as if my insides had been sucked out. "That sounds like a nightmare."

It all makes sense. Kaipo, trembling in the driveway of the home he couldn't go back to. That scream of grief and frustration on those cliffs.

And those intrusive thoughts. Just like mine. Those angry replays of what happened to me, keeping me stuck in an endless loop of agitation.

Fangs sinking into flesh. Volok's cruel laughter. The hair-raising screeching of rats.

Goose bumps pop out all over me.

Kaipo nods, swallowing down the tears in his throat. "There wasn't anything there for me anymore, so I left. Became a Navy diver to find a new family. Did underwater welding, salvage, combat missions. And for a time, I was happy, I think. One by one, though, I lost my buddies."

All those friends in that photo . . .

He shakes his head. "And I couldn't bear losing another family. So I left the Navy, too. I didn't know if I'd ever find a way to love myself again. That is, until I found freediving." A disbelieving smile crinkles his eyes, and he shuts them, trying to find the words. "When you're on a breath hold, everything falls away. It's just you and the water. It's . . . timeless." He draws in a long, peaceful breath. "There's no room for intrusive thoughts down there. You *have* to be present, or you die. I'm safe there. I can feel alive again. The trauma can't find me. And I began to be happy again. Somehow, bit by bit, I found a way to live with the pain. To enjoy things. To make jokes. To laugh. To love." He looks down at my hand in his. "Deep down, I'm terrified of being abandoned again. And I'm working on that. So when I woke, and you were there, and you'd fought for me . . ." His eyes skitter away from mine. They're very glassy. "I wish . . ." he croaks.

"What?" I ask, breathless.

He meets my eyes. "I wish I had someone who was as loyal as you."

My heart clenches. *I don't know if I'm as loyal as you think.*

"But you do," I say, and smile, trying not to let my fangs show too much. "We're friends now, aren't we?"

He gives me a look. "You know what I mean." The timbre of his voice changes, grows softer. "I really admire that about you. You've spent centuries fighting for your husband, and you've never given up. Reinhard's a lucky man."

A lucky man.

I look away, not sure if I can bear to meet the admiration in his gaze right now.

I miss Reinhard. I do. But even though I miss him, it's starting to get hard to really *remember* him. Over so many years, I've forgotten what he smells like. The sound of his voice. The way it felt to be in his arms.

Right now, everything is Kaipo.

He's like the sun. How can I be expected to recall anything about Reinhard, when Kaipo Kalawai'a is blazing right in front of me?

I feel something within me wobble, and know that if I don't put a stop to this, I'm going to fall.

I pull my hand out of Kaipo's and look away. "You should get some sleep. We have a lot of travel ahead of us."

There's a silence, and I can feel his eyes on me, but I don't turn to look at him.

"Okay," he says at last, the hurt and confusion plain in his voice. It's like a stab to my heart. "Good night."

He brushes past me and climbs down the ladder. It's only when I hear a sliding door open and close that I let out a breath and tip my head back to look at the stars, my eyes burning.

# SEVENTEEN

It takes us ten days to get there.

We thread our way through the Malacca Strait, across the Andaman Sea and into the Arabian Sea, hitting squally weather along the way. We hear reports of Somali pirates, but encounter none.

That's not the threat we're worried about, though.

We gain the southern entrance to the Red Sea at midday. A strait called the Bab al-Mandab. The Gate of Tears. So called because the wind and water, no matter the time of year, are always against you.

When I glance astern, I see—far off on the windblown wavetops—the flash of boat hulls. Three of them.

Maybe pursuing us. Maybe not.

Maybe with burgees fluttering from their bows, black and emblazoned with a green V.

We transit into the Red Sea.

It is another world in that passage, unchanged since the birth of man. Lazy golden sands. Turquoise water glittering with light. White-sailed boats glide up and down the wide river of a sea, old dhows harkening back to the time of the Ottomans. They share the lanes with modern superyachts cruising the Red Sea for dive sites or berths at the glitzy resorts dotting the coastline. Here and there, lovely pots of water also glimmer along the coast, beautiful marsa anchorages that shimmer like a mirage. They're ringed by the bones and petrified hides of animals that came out of the desert to slake their thirst there, realizing only too late that it was saltwater.

And all the while, those three boats follow.

A leaden anxiety sets in as we cruise up the strait. Behind us, the three boats pick up speed, too. Kaipo and I glance at each other.

"They could be pirates?" I say, scrunching up my forehead and shrugging one shoulder.

Kaipo lifts a droll brow. "Really?"

I roll my eyes and take a moment, squinting. With my unnaturally sharp eyesight, distance shrinks in a vertiginous widening of the senses, the Red Sea and Gate of Tears seeming to rush toward me, bearing those boat hulls closer, making them clearer. They're composed of fiberglass. And they're white.

I straighten, blinking at the strain on my eyes. "They're yachts."

Kaipo nods, as if having expected this. "Hang on," he says.

He fulcrums the throttle forward and the stern thrusters hum, lurching us into sickening flight. China rattles in its cabinets. Spume mists the air. And behind us, the three yachts match our speed.

There is no doubt now of who they are.

We are being hunted.

I turn to Kaipo at the wheel. "What do we do if they catch up to us?"

He gives me a grim look, a light sweat gleaming on his brow. "I have guns onboard. But in my experience, against them . . ."

My insides squirm into knots.

As the *Kanaloa* galumphs across the waves, I slip out onto the shaded lee of the starboard side to look behind us again. The yachts are gaining on us. They're not a quarter mile off our stern now, burgees clearly fluttering from their bows, sickly green Vs gleaming on a black field.

Reinhard's face comes into my head, the thought of being dragged back to Transmarinia, and the panic begins to set in. I sweep the coastlines with my gaze, looking for a place to hide. Somewhere. Anywhere. But we can't. Not with them so close on our tail.

Perhaps we can get help. Perhaps someone else is out here who can—

But there's no one. The sea has gone dark and gray, shadowed by clouds rolling in. There's not a boat in sight.

No resort anywhere. No boat anywhere. The dhows long gone, the diving yachts put into port. It's only us and our pursuers out here.

And something else. There's a light tinkling, red particles dancing along the teak and fiberglass of the *Kanaloa*. Grit blows into my eyes.

And shielding my eyes, I lift them to the sky again.

There's something wrong with those clouds rolling in off the Sahara. They're gargantuan, biblical, suffused with color.

They're orange.

"Kaipo?" I hazard in a wary voice.

The fisherman nods, eyes also on the horizon. "I see it." He guns the throttle to the max. "We might just be in luck."

"What do you m—" But the question dies on my lips as I see the sand whirling up into the sky like a plague, blotting out the sun and covering the Red Sea in a hand of darkness.

It's a sandstorm.

My stomach drops. "Mein Gott," I breathe. "You think we can hide in that?"

Kaipo flashes me a mad, infectious grin.

I glance behind. The yachts are frighteningly close, gliding abreast of us on both sides. And there are crew members on deck. Anonymous in black sunglasses, black polos. They heft long coils of rope in their hands, barbed and glinting at the ends: grappling hooks.

*"Kaipo!"* I scream.

He yanks the helm over hard a'port, and grappling hooks fall short and splash into the sea. Then I'm clutching the rail, the whole length of the *Kanaloa* shuddering as it crashes into the boat on our port side, bashing her out of the way.

*Clunk, clunk.* More grappling hooks, clattering onto the deck and sucking back to catch against the rail. The

*Kanaloa* starts to veer off-course as the Sons of Volok deckhands begin to reel her in, straining her engine.

"Ilsa!" Kaipo shouts.

I'm already on it. I snatch a wide-bladed fishing knife out of its sheath on the wheelhouse wall, dash out onto the gangway and hack away at the grappling hooks. They're monstrously thick, my knife bouncing off them in painstaking snappings of twine. I cast a glance ahead.

A wall of orange looms, a wrathful howling of sand. So close.

The Sons of Volok boat on our starboard closes the gap in a creaking of rope, almost fender to fender. The deckhands crouch, ready to spring aboard.

*"Ilsa?!"*

The last rope parts with a twang. "Now!"

The *Kanaloa* jerks free and Kaipo guns it, blasting us ahead—and straight into the sandstorm.

The world turns orange. Headwinds howl into me with vicious force, staggering me back a few steps. I go blind. Sand needles into my cheeks, my upraised arms, stoppering up my ears. I fall to my knees, groping for the wheelhouse and struggling not to cough, lips pressed tight against smothering grit. I can't even call out Kaipo's name for help.

But he's there suddenly, strong hands pulling me inside. I hear the wheelhouse door slide closed and the howling is muted to a plaintive roar. Then he's wiping gently at my eyes with a wet cloth and I blink.

The world is a restless, rust-colored blizzard outside. It moans and shrieks, desert sand tapping and tinkling against the glass, obscuring everything into a billowing shroud.

No sign of the Sons of Volok boats anywhere.

"Are we good?" I find myself asking, my throat raw and weak. "Are we safe here?"

"Yeah, we're good." But Kaipo isn't scanning the windows for shapes in the gloom; he's peering at me with something like concern.

"That's good."

"Ilsa?" Kaipo asks, and touches my arm. "You okay?"

"Of course," I grumble with a flash of annoyance, my brow furrowing in a frown. "Why wouldn't I be?"

We're good. We're safe now. There's nothing to worry about.

I'm still thinking this as I collapse, and the world goes dark.

# EIGHTEEN

A face looms above me. It's a blur at first, all sharp angles, thick sideburns framing prominent cheekbones. Then eyes like the blue heart of a fire.

My chest tightens.

"Reinhard," I breathe, smiling, and lift a hand.

But I don't touch that face. It wavers and blurs and takes shape again, turning into—

"Hey," Kaipo says, holding my wrist as his mouth twists in an unhappy slant. "It's me."

Embarrassment floods my face. "Where—" I start, trying to force myself up. "What—"

But he pushes me back down. "Hush. Take it easy."

"What happened—"

"You had a fall."

"A fall." I touch the back of my head and wince. It's throbbing.

"I think . . ." He swallows, his mouth tight. "I think you haven't . . ."

"Fed." I shut my eyes, suddenly aware of the parched rawness in my throat and feeling like a fool. *Of course.* "I haven't fed in weeks."

He nods. "You've been out for most of the day."

"Most of the—" I look about. I'm in his cabin—his bed—his scent all around me. It's dim in here; it must be night.

When I look at him again, he's pushing up the sleeve of the rugged Henley he's wearing.

Every muscle in my body clenches. "What are you doing?"

"You need to feed," he says, as if stating the obvious, and presses his wrist to my lips.

I scramble back against the headboard, nostrils flared. "Don't."

He freezes, wrist outheld, his brow crinkled in a frown. "Why?"

"Because—don't you understand—" I can't even get the words out; my cold cheeks are aflame. The thought of sinking my teeth into his vein fills me with horror and criminal joy.

"What don't I understand—"

But I'm looking away, anywhere than at his offered wrist, his flesh, the delicious quiver of blood there. "Put us ashore. I'll go hunt—"

But he sighs, throwing out a hand. "You mean in this? We can't go anywhere while this storm is raging."

And it *is* still raging. It's been there all along: the low roar of the wind, the ticking of sand against the hull and superstructures. The sandstorm, trapping us out here on the Red Sea.

I swallow, feeling cornered and flushed in a feverish slick of sweat. I didn't even know my kind could sweat. "Then we'll wait."

His sigh is impatient now, frustrated. "Ilsa, we don't know how long it'll last—"

"We'll wait, I said." And I burrow down into the covers and wrap them around me, shivering and trying to block out the beat of his blood in my ears.

My sleep is restless. It takes me a long time to finally slip into its dark embrace. And when I do, I burn, wracked with hunger and despair. I claw at the sheets, bunch them in my fists as my body is tormented with a thirst that is ruthless, all-consuming.

And always I find Kaipo there, sitting on the edge of the bed with a cool cloth pressed to my brow.

Kind Kaipo. Warm Kaipo. His forearm thickly corded with muscle and throbbing with blood . . .

I brush the cloth away. "You shouldn't be near me."

He smirks, seemingly amused by this warning.

But he doesn't know. He doesn't understand.

I writhe in the sheets, feet sliding about, toes curling. Sweat slicks my skin, sticking my clothes and hair to me. My head is on fire. My breasts ache. And down there, between my legs, another furious desire . . .

I whimper, hips grinding helplessly against the mattress, and there's a hand on my shoulder.

"Ilsa?" He leans close, his heavy musk in my nostrils, shredding all my thoughts to rags. "Ilsa? Talk to me—"

I don't recall moving. But next I know, I've gripped his Henley by both hands and pulled him down toward me, forcing him to brace himself over me with one hand on either side of me on the mattress, caging me in.

I freeze.

He blinks at me, his eyes enormous as I pant into his face. My lips are peeled back in a snarl, and his eyes drop to my fangs, linger on my lips.

He's not afraid.

His gaze lifts to mine again. There's no flinching on his part, no instinct toward self-preservation at all.

He's fine with whatever happens next.

I can't hear anything. So close, his heartbeats boom like thunderclaps. A vein throbs on his neck, thick and defenseless. And his lips—they glow with color, made to be kissed, punctured, sucked on.

My fangs ache.

My eye twitches.

My thighs squirm with pleasure.

I ache up toward him, fangs poised long and curved. Our lips are less than an inch apart, almost grazing each other. We breathe into each other's mouths.

And I think: *Reinhard*.

In one explosive movement, I fling Kaipo away with violent strength, shove all two hundred pounds of him across the room and through a closet door in a splintering of boards. *"Stay away from me!"*

The boat rocks, the creaking of wood like a dirge. I can hear howling. Reinhard screaming. Or maybe that's a storm. The sandstorm.

That's right. I'm still on the Red Sea, my consciousness drifting in and out of sleep like the melody of a dying song.

Here and there, moments of clarity, horrible lucidity.

"You keep saying his name."

I blink through a haze of fever, sensing the delicacy with which this voice is tiptoeing around this. The closet door hangs askew, its boards bright with a network of cracks, unvarnished wood showing through. And in front of it, haunted and haggard, Kaipo sits in a chair on the far side of the bed like a good boy, keeping his distance from me.

He lowers an icepack from where he'd been holding it to the back of his head, studies it in his big hands. "He must be a good man."

I try to swallow the desert in my throat. Did I do that to him? "He is." My cracked lips flicker in a smile. "Is this how you find out about my husband? By taking advantage of me in my moment of weakness?"

His mouth crooks, but there's no mirth in it. He looks like a man who wants to ask a question but dreads hearing the answer. He asks anyway. "What made you fall in love with him?"

I consider shutting him down, fending off this inquiry with some dry statement, but I can't. Not with him.

I take a breath. "He helped me become what I never thought I could be."

Our eyes lock, and for a moment I no longer know to whom I'm referring.

Over and over, it comes to me. The thought of giving in and feeding on Kaipo. And every time I push it away, burying my face into the pillow.

*Later*, I tell myself. *I can't think about that now. I can't think about it at all. It's forbidden.*

*I'm not that. I can't be that.*

*That would be disloyalty. That would be cheating.*

*That is adultery.*

But in sleep, there's no defense against my thoughts. With traitorous honesty they present my situation to me in all its stark ugliness. One dream visits me above all others, over and over. I dream that they're both my husbands, that they both lavish their love on me. Reinhard weeps, kissing my hands and saying: "Be at peace, dear. I forgive you! Look how happy we all are!" And Kaipo is there also, and he smiles as he offers me his bleeding wrists where my fangs have marked them. And kneeling and suckling from one and then the other, I marvel that this had once seemed impossible to me. This union. This happiness. And we all laugh, smeared in blood and teeth shining, and I tell them that this is much simpler now, isn't it? And I wake in the smothering sheets with my throat blocked up with horror.

"Hush, Ilsa. Hush."

But I can't stop weeping. I am clawing at him in febrile panic.

"No, no . . . I'm awful . . . I'm *unclean* . . . Leave me alone!"

But his arms—Kaipo's arms—are around me, holding me close. "Never," comes his whispered reply.

Later, more ravings, more confessions.

"It's my fault . . . All my fault . . ."

"*What?* Why?"

"If I hadn't gained a reputation as a shipwright, they wouldn't have come after us . . ."

"Who?"

"The horrors . . . the fanged one . . . Volok . . ."

"What are you saying?"

"None of it would have happened . . . Reinhard would be free, if I'd known my place . . ."

"Your place?"

"As a woman . . . I outshone my husband . . . I spurned my station . . . I was ungrateful . . . A wicked, wicked woman . . ."

Silence.

Then: "Ilsa? That's not true. You did nothing wrong. You can't blame yourself. Do you hear me? *You can't blame yourself.*"

My eyes: hot, wet, leaking. "And now I can't let it go. I can't let *him* go . . . even if I wanted to . . ."

And then something on my eyes—Reinhard's lips, Kaipo's lips—kissing the tears away.

"Ilsa? Ilsa! You have to feed. Do you hear me?"

When I flutter my eyes open, I have never seen Kaipo so afraid. His face is pale and trembling.

A small part of me triumphs in this concern for me, and my eyes slide closed again.

"Ilsa!"

I groan. I'm so tired. So very tired. I just want to shut my eyes . . .

But Kaipo won't let me.

He hauls me upright in bed and shakes me by the shoulders. I grimace, head lolling, and then there's a stinging smack to my cheek that flies my eyes wide open.

He's slapped me.

"You're wasting away. Do you hear me? You . . ." His eyes trail down me, horrified. "You barely weigh a thing. You need blood. Now. Before . . ."

And I am wasting away. When I lift my arms, they look as if they belong to someone else. A withered mummy. Something dead. And then I remember that I am.

My laugh comes out a croak.

Kaipo glares at me, eyes sparking. "You want to find your husband?" He leans in, teeth gritted. "Then you need to feed."

Slowly, weakly, I shake my head. "You don't understand. When you feed on someone you—"

"What? Someone you what?"

But I bite my lip.

His curse isn't soft. "I promised Arie. I promised her I'd take care of you. *Don't you lose her*, she said. And I'll be damned if I will. Now." He brandishes his wrist under my nose. "Fucking *bite me*."

We lock eyes. Something charges between us. My heart swells.

I can't do this. How could I live with myself afterward? And how could I leave Reinhard to his fate?

"Ilsa," Kaipo orders, or maybe it's a plea.

When I don't move, he sighs, giving his head a disappointed little sideways tilt, and taking out a knife he slits his wrist.

# NINETEEN

It takes me a moment to realize I've sunk my teeth into Kaipo's open wrist, and that my mouth is filled with his blood.

My whole body convulses with the force of me sucking it down, and my irises blow out, sensation exploding inside me, my nerves going off like fireworks. It's unlike anything I've ever tasted. Nothing like that rancid ex-con in Florida, or those grimy riders on the transport ship. No. It's because it's . . .

Kaipo.

Yes, his blood has that spicy tang of new-poured iron. But it also tastes like his scent, and his smile, and his tattoos. Like the way he jokes and gets me out of a bad mood, and gets serious when he looks at me. It tastes of his pain and his loneliness, and a deep yearning for something he cannot have. His blood tastes of everything that makes up what he is, and he is sharing it with me.

It's dizzying, and overwhelming, and exquisite, and terrifying.

Far away, I hear Kaipo hiss in a breath, not entirely out of pain, and I barely hear him. His blood has hit me like a tide, rapturously delicious, the most delicious thing I can imagine, and I have drowned.

"Ilsa," he grunts.

Warm. I can't remember the last time I felt warm. It's like a fever. A beautiful, burning heat. And his blood is hitting my stomach now, kickstarting a dynamite fuse of resurrection crackling along my synapses. My nerves spark. My capillaries bloom. My wasted limbs round out, life returning to my undead body. I have been reborn.

And still I drink.

I should stop, I know. I'm drinking too much. I could kill him. But a frightening voracity has been awoken in me, and stopping now seems as impossible as facing the dawn. I have become one solid core of need.

I need more. I need Kaipo to be closer. I want to climb inside his flesh. I want to gorge on the pulsing meat of his heart. I want, want, *want*.

"Ilsa," Kaipo breathes, begging.

Somehow, I tear myself away and look up into his eyes, an apology poised on my wet lips.

And yes, he's pale. Dangerously so. But his mouth is parted in longing. "More," he says, his voice rough and guttural, and tangling his fingers in the storm of hair at my nape, he pulls me to him again.

My heart sings.

I don't return to his wrist. And that's not where he's pulling me, anyway. My hands hike up onto his shoulders and I pull myself onto him, legs wrapping around his waist as his hands cup my ass, and letting out a soft whimper of need I nuzzle at his neck, the tips of my canines finding the rushing warmth of a vein there, and bite down.

The fount of hot life is exquisite. Kaipo lets out a moan and cradles my head deeper into the crook of his neck. "Ilsa. *Ilsa.*" Kneeling there in the bed, he bucks against me in a way that does not feel fully within his control. "Take it. Take all you want . . ."

I hum a blissful moan into his skin: I'm not going anywhere. I'd rather die again. Something wet and eager bursts inside me, spills into my stomach, and I cling to him, one hand on his shoulder, the other buried in his golden-brown curls, my own hair falling like a veil of silver across him. I am gorging on him like a nightmare out of a painting.

"Ilsa." My name, in his mouth, sounds like a prayer or a curse, something both holy and filthy. His fingertips press into the flesh of my ass, and I press myself to him, desperate for contact. For something to touch. To fit against. My hips grind against his lap, and when I feel how hard he is, something thrums throughout my entire body. I need *more.*

Before I know it, I'm grinding on him and whimpering into his neck, and his breath is a hoarse pant in my ear as he thrusts against me, trying to find that perfect spot to welcome him. I almost lose my place in his vein and pull myself back with a needy, babyish whimper. I can feel his blood dripping from my mouth, down my chin. I'm wet everywhere, every atom in my body alive and glowing. And he's speaking to me.

"Ilsa, if you keep going, I'm going to—fuck." His voice drops, rough and reverent, full of awe. "Yes," he breathes as I move against him, my throat bobbing greedily as I suck him down. He hisses in a breath. "That's it, that's it," he coos. Urging. Commanding. "That's my good girl . . ."

That does it. The tingling pleasure shoots through me so suddenly, so forcefully, my thighs clamp down and my nails claw into his skin. My back bows, but I hold on, moaning, still buried in his vein. Then something gives way and the orgasm explodes inside me, rolling my eyes back into my head, knocking the wind from me. The pleasure is searing, world-breaking. An ecstasy of terrible joy. It rolls through me, unstoppable, as bright as the dawn, and I come, and come, and come, wrung out and blinded in an obliteration of bliss. The fulfillment of it—the *rawness* of it—is almost scary, as if this sexual experience had been the first, a breakthrough into a new, sparkling world.

Eventually it subsides and I sag in Kaipo's arms, the lazy aftershocks leaving me twitching and quivering, my whole body pulsing.

And still, I'm latched to his neck, my fangs nestled in his vein.

I don't think about it—guided by some primordial instinct, I slide my fangs out of him and begin to lick at the wounds I opened, lapping up every last drop of blood. It is deliciously erotic. I am lost, in a trance. Satiated and plumped up with happiness. I am content in a way I cannot remember ever feeling before. I feel safe.

Licking my lips, I lean back to look into his pale face drained of all color, his hooded eyes—the curiosity, arousal, and satisfaction there.

And I remember: Kaipo. Not Reinhard.

The room quivers.

He seems to understand the expression on my face. His own falls. "I didn't know that—I had no idea it would be like—that."

I slide back off his lap, and he lets me. He raises his hands. "Ilsa, I'm so sorry—"

But I'm shaking my head and quailing away from his touch, sliding off the bed and onto the floor. He gapes. "*Ilsa*—"

"Mein Gott. Mein Gott, forgive me," I whisper, my bottom lip quivering, and put my hands to my face. I don't even know to whom I'm speaking. "Forgive me! Forgive me!"

"Ilsa. Ilsa!" he keeps saying, kneeling to grab my forearms. "What—"

But I cannot look at him. All the warmth I had been plumped up with just a moment before is now gone. I have been plunged into guilt and cold despair.

"Don't look at me. Don't touch me. *Get away from me!*"

I feel his body retreat. His voice wavers, filled with hurt. "But—but that was—for me, that was—"

"Don't!" I whisper, pleading, shaking my head. "It didn't happen. Don't ever speak of it. Not ever."

"Okay," he whispers, desperate to soothe me. "Okay."

He places his hands on his hips and paces, waiting it out with me. Unable to leave me. But still, I cannot look at him. I cannot bear to put into words this wonderful and terrible entry into a new life. This new understanding of what I am. What I am capable of. To do so would only trivialize this feeling now within me, and I cannot do that. I cannot reduce this event with clumsy, imprecise language. It would be a disgrace to Reinhard's memory. It would be a disgrace to what I have just shared with this beautiful man. It would be a disgrace to all that is within my soul.

I must keep it within me, this shameful price of my joy, and never speak of it. This transgression. This miracle. This lovely sin.

But Kaipo, it seems, needs to speak.

He slides his hands down his face and looks at me. "I don't know if I can do this."

I raise my head from my knees, my stomach dropping at his tone. "What do you mean?"

"I don't—" He makes an awkward, abortive gesture and rubs the back of his neck. "I don't know if I can go on helping you anymore."

My voice has gone low and flat. "Why?"

"Because . . ." He stares at me, helpless. "Don't you know? I'm *falling* for you, Ilsa. I *have* fallen for you."

I blink. My face has turned to pins and needles.

"I don't know how you did it, frankly." He snorts. "You're the prickliest, proudest, most infuriating person

I've ever met. By all accounts, we shouldn't even get along. You hate jokes. You're a perfectionist. You don't listen. You're as stubborn as a lug nut and just as overtightened. But goddamn if I don't love it. You've torched your way past all my defenses and I can't stop thinking about you. I'm obsessed with you, Ilsa. Even with the two of us trapped on this boat together, I still can't get near enough to you. Somehow, you've become my entire world. And finding your husband means I'll lose you. And I don't know if I could survive that."

I stare at him, my face hot, spun into a state of breathless suspension at this confession. I was not ready for this. If only he knew what his words were doing to me.

When I finally speak, I feel like a child, small and lost. "So you're just going to leave."

He shakes his head, anguished, and notices his hands are shaking. He laughs. "I think my abandonment issues are kicking in. I don't know if I—"

"Then you should go."

His head jerks up. "Ilsa—"

"Go!" I snap. I'm trembling, too. Every instinct in me screaming to retreat, shut down, put my walls up again. I've been duped, tricked into opening my heart after all this time. And so that old anger takes over. "*Go!*" I snarl. "I'll be fine. I've always done it on my own. Why would I need someone now? I never wanted you to come along, anyway."

Kaipo blinks, his mouth working as he pushes down the hurt in his face. "At least take the *Kanaloa*—"

I scoff. "I won't take her from you. Just—take me ashore and I'll buy another boat."

He lingers, the muscles dancing in his jaw as his hands bunch at his sides. He looks as if he wants to speak, and I'm not sure if I want him to. Then he slips out the door and it clicks shut behind him.

# TWENTY

In the morning the sandstorm passes, and we find the *Kanaloa* has been turned orange.

It's everywhere. A sifting of iron-oxide red covers the teak and fiberglass, clings to the grease on the winches, windlass, and roller chocks. She looks as if she's done battle with the elements.

From the shade of the starboard gangway, Kaipo studies his boat, a pained look on his face. I know what that expression means. That sandstorm would have aged the *Kanaloa* by years, the wear and tear on her terrible. He should be washing her down now to avoid as much damage as he can.

But he doesn't. He merely turns back into the wheelhouse and starts the engines.

This makes it harder, much harder, for me to ignore a twinge of sympathy for him. I can't bear to see him look this defeated. This wounded.

But I cut that off with merciless force. I can't allow myself to think that way about him right now. I can't allow myself to think of him at all.

I must hold onto this shame to keep me to my course. To stick to this decision that with every passing moment feels more and more ruinous.

But more importantly, I must hold onto what has served me so well all these years:

Rage.

Yes. That I can use. That I don't have to feel guilty about.

When I've changed back into my gray business suit, Kaipo's clothes he lent me left folded on his bed, I stand on a shaded gangway and watch land approach.

The *Kanaloa* was not the only thing affected by the storm. Everywhere, the Red Sea is covered in a fine layer of Saharan sand, giving it a surreal, reddish-tinged haze. The palm trees along the banks have been ravaged, their fronds blown across dunes that have been whipped into new shapes, their crests as delicate and elegant as a calligrapher's brush strokes. The sails of the listing boats at anchor have been blown as ragged as the trees. Even the glitzy resort we're approaching is covered in sand, boys in white uniforms sweeping flurries of red off its dock.

And it's getting closer.

I shift my weight, clearing my throat with effort. A growing panic is crowding my windpipe. A sense of doom. Of catastrophic regret. But we're already gliding up to the dock and Kaipo is standing at the bow, tossing a mooring line to one of the boys in uniform. It's happening. It's all happening so fast. Kaipo is lowering the passerelle onto the dock and then he's standing aside and turning to me, waiting. I walk up to him, my umbrella carefully angled to shield my skin from the blazing sun. I look up into his face. His jaw is clamped down, the hurt radiating from his very pores. This is my chance. I could take back what I said. I could admit I was wrong. I could fight for us.

Do it. Now.

But I don't.

He sees it in my face. He smiles, that humor I thought could never be repressed tamped down to a low, sour flame. Then he dips his head below the canopy of my umbrella and places his lips to my brow, letting the tenderness of that touch linger until I have to shut my eyes to hide the prickling heat behind them.

I fight down a sob.

"Take care, Shipwright," he whispers against my brow.

"Take care, Fishman."

Then he's leaning away and I'm somehow walking on, somehow marching down the passerelle onto the dock with the white-uniformed boys capering around me, offering me hotel rooms, souvenirs, baksheesh! And when I've glanced back Kaipo has already turned away, huge shoulders slumped. And then the *Kanaloa* is reversing away from the dock and turning into the Red Sea, bearing him away to Mexico maybe, to Cozumel and retirement, and a life without me.

And then he's gone.

It doesn't take long to find another boat. There are a lot of them moored near the resort, and I have plenty of Arie's money to spend. I consider hiring on the captain, but the thought of sailing with a person who is not Kaipo—someone who does not have his bantering voice, his rakish smile, his comforting calm—fills me with a wild, desolate anger that scares me. "Just the boat, please," I snap, snatching the keys from the owner's hand.

Getting the 30-foot cruiser yacht disembarked is a mortifying affair. My handling of the bow thrusters is terrible, and my face is hot with embarrassment as the fenders squeak, threatening to pop as my starboard side drags along the dock. I've attracted a small crowd by the time I'm in open water.

Once I'm in the starboard lane heading upcoast, I put the boat on autopilot and look over at the atlas in its tube on the chart table. At the empty wheelhouse around me. Its walls with no fishing equipment. Its paneling with no charmingly rough edges. And it finally hits me like a hammer-blow to the gut.

I slide down against the helm, my arms wrapped around my drawn-up knees, and burst into sobs as I whisper Kaipo's name.

# TWENTY-ONE

I press on up the Red Sea in a dream. The countries on the western shore slowly turn into Eritrea, then Sudan, and finally Egypt. I travel mostly by night and sleep during the day, dropping anchor in some private cove and hoping I don't wake to the sound of sinister footsteps abovedeck.

Every time I spot a yacht, I'm caught between dread that it's the Sons of Volok and hope that it's Kaipo.

I know I'm being childish. He has no reason to come back. I'm taken. I'm *married*. I can't give him what he wants. And I wouldn't be able to live with myself knowing I was putting him through that kind of abandonment terror.

He deserves better.

He deserves a woman who can give all of herself to him, and not what little traitorous part of me has so far. He deserves to be happy.

The thought of him with someone else makes my stomach turn over.

As the days and nights bleed together, a great darkness settles over me, sapping my strength. I stand at the helm, listless. During the day, I lie face down on the bed in the master suite without undressing, my arms folded, my head resting on them. I feel a great weight pressing down on my body, smothering me. My head is heavy. My arms stones. A flickershow of images shuttle through my mind with queasy rapidity: Kaipo laughing, Kaipo smiling, Kaipo joking, the way Kaipo would look at me, Kaipo's vulnerability as he shared his family history with me, the way Kaipo groaned my name as I fed from him, the way Kaipo stared at me open-mouthed as I came on his lap.

Kaipo, Kaipo, Kaipo.

I cannot sleep; I toss and turn all day, bereft and despairing. I thought I had known depression. I thought I had known loss with my husband. I cannot even think it—it feels like a sin to compare them—but I've felt this before. The knowledge settles in my gut, hard and immutable: This is heartbreak. This is the breaking of a heart.

The slow, inexorable hollowing, the pain that brings you to the edge and then recedes, leaving you stranded on a plain of lethargy. You get to a place where you're convinced you cannot bear it, that this agitation, this frenzy of despair clawing its way up out of you will be the end of all. A grand and almost implausible height of emotion. And then, day by day, you find that it is in fact bearable. That we are, in the end, conceited creatures, to believe that such fleeting passions will endure. Eventually, time will grind them out, leave you flattened and pulsing with a dull pang of loss. It will never be debilitating, never unmanageable, but it also will never not be there, either. An indefatigable, almost boring monotony of hurt that you will both curse and cherish, because it reminds you of him.

Maybe I'm a fool. A vain, spoiled little fool. Who am I to think I'm so special? Maybe what we shared wasn't so special to him. Maybe he's already forgotten about me. Maybe it was all in my head.

Does he miss me now? Is he having the same thoughts? Is he as tortured with loss as I am? Will he be as haunted as I will be by him?

By late afternoon, I give up trying to sleep and ascend to the wheelhouse, get the yacht underway. White shimmers on the horizon, and I straighten at the helm, my heart in my throat. But it's only one of the dhows, its lateen sails billowing mockingly in the breeze.

I settle back onto my heels and glare at the single-masted ship as it passes, the sea gypsies at the gunwales who wave to me with great cheer. I know I should feed again, but I can't. I don't want to lose the taste of Kaipo's blood on my tongue.

On the seventh day I wake at dusk to find a storm rolling in.

No sandstorm, this one. But a bruiser, dark thunderheads soon whipping hard peltings of rain almost sideways over the Red Sea. It lashes the windows, drums against the roof, tipping my yacht dangerously in the deep troughs. Soon windblown spume is slapping against the wheelhouse in great waves, reducing my visibility to almost nothing. The world is a heaving black tantrum.

I'm considering dropping anchor and riding it out when lightning flares far off over the sea, footing a jagged bolt of white to the waves that illuminates a ship adrift out there.

My skin contracts. A chill wraps around the base of my spine.

I squint.

It's dead in the water, buffeted by the waves with its lights off. But in the flashes of lightning, I can see it has a familiar profile. A sloped superstructure with a tuna tower. An aft deck arch of fishing rods.

The *Kanaloa*.

Adrenaline hums in my veins.

I ramp up the throttle and steer for her. There's a high-pitched whine in my ears. What happened to him? Is he riding it out? Was there an accident?

Was he ambushed by the Sons of Volok while he was coming back for me?

My heart strains in my chest.

The bow of my yacht dips sickeningly into a trough and spume cascades onto the wheelhouse windshield. When it froths away, I squint at the boat again. I can make out the worn gilt lettering on its transom. It reads *Quarry*.

Not the *Kanaloa*. Not Kaipo. Just another sportfishing yacht.

Oh.

I shut my eyes. I feel faint, the floor lurching beneath me more than it should. The mixture of relief and disappointment is dizzying.

But still. The boat looks damaged. In danger. I have to help.

I put my yacht into stationary mode, pull on a black wetsuit I bought before disembarking, and dive off the swim deck into the sea.

The water is freezing, breath-stealing, making me gasp from the cold. And strong. But I'm stronger. I cut through the suck and heave of the waves and slap a hand up onto the bobbing swim deck of the fishing yacht, then the other, haul myself dripping aboard.

It's deserted. The deck swept clean of sea gear, the fishing poles trembling like antennae in the wind. The tuna tower empty. At aft a crane, its arm swung over the stern with a steel cable descending from it into the water, thrumming from the strain. No souls to be seen.

Maybe they're huddling in the cabin.

I stagger across the aft deck, feeling my way along the saltscoured rail against the slant of the boat, water surging through the scuppers to foam around my bare feet. The cabin door rattles back, the lock broken. Inside, the helm unmanned, water rushing in tides across the floor and dripping belowdeck. I take a few steps closer to the stair landing, pushing myself off the bulkheads against the tilt, and peer down. A glimpse of wet papers and trash floating in the dark water, life jackets among the seepage. It looks as if it's been ransacked.

But no bodies.

"Hello?" I call, listening for movement. "Anyone here?"

No answer. Woodwork creaks. Pipes groan. A sour dampness reaches my nostrils.

I don't want to go down there.

I back away, gooseflesh creeping up my back. I no longer want to be here. I no longer want to be on this boat.

Pirates. Yes. It must have been pirates. That's all.

Wouldn't they have commandeered the boat, though? Wouldn't they have left people aboard?

There's an obvious answer lurking there. But I'm not ready to face that yet.

I lurch out of the cabin and stop. Before me looms the crane, a black arm against the flare of lightning. I don't want to, but I press the button and watch the cable winch up, reeling in whatever it's attached to.

It rises slick and dripping out of the sea. Huge, metallic, glinting in the wet gloom. A shark diving cage, its steel bars pried open by some terrible force so something could get inside. And things my mind can't make sense of dangle from its bottom, as languid as seaweed or the boneless arms of squid.

In the following strike of lightning, I see what those things are. They're arms. Soft, pallid, sparkly nails flashing. And those arms belong to the bodies of women filling the cage. A whole heap of them. Slumped, drained white with fang marks all over them, their eyes bulging in horror.

And something's in there with them. Something crouched over them in a drenched business suit. It lifts its head to look at me, gobbets of flesh dripping from its chin, and in the following flash of lightning its eyes glow to cold silver discs and it smiles a sharp and bloody smile at me.

The world veers beneath my feet.

A trap. It was a trap all along.

I turn to the portside gunwale to flee, but there's something already clambering out of the sea to crouch there like some goatish horror. Something with sharp teeth and glowing eyes. And when I whirl to the starboard rail, a vision is appearing out of the flickerings of lightning like some dread vessel of old: a cruiser yacht with a burgee fluttering at its bow jackstaff. The burgee has a green V emblazoned on its black field.

They've found me. They've come.

A wave broadsides the sportfishing yacht, tipping up its bow, and miscellaneous sea gear slides out of the open cabin and down the tilting deck. A foulweather jacket. Coils of braided cable. A first aid kit. And something else, washing up at my feet like a blessing.

A flaregun.

I don't think. I snatch it up, point it at the thing crouching on the rail and pull the trigger.

The flare rockets up in a white arc and blasts the thing off the rail. One moment it's there, and the other it's simply gone. A flash of hot tendrils of magnesium hanging in the air, the acrid smell of burnt flesh. But I don't linger to watch. I'm already moving, stepping up onto the gunwale and launching myself into the sea.

Crushing cold, and then I'm surfacing and stroking hard and fast, a booming in my ears. I can hear beastly snarls of rage behind me that freeze the blood in my veins. And then splashes. Sounds of pursuit.

Lord save me.

I clamber onto the swim deck of my yacht and stagger down the gangway, bouncing off the rail in the heavings of spray, and haul back the wheelhouse door.

A dripping shadow stands at the helm like some damned captain dredged from the ocean depths, holding the plastic drafting tube containing the atlas. There's a rumble of thunder and lightning catches in the pinpricks of its eyes. It smiles. "Hello, Shipwright." It waggles the tube. "Looking for this?"

Horror closes my throat. My eyes drop to the drafting tube, and so does the Son of Volok's.

A wave staggers us both, and I take my chance—I snatch a leather case of binoculars off a shelf and wallop the Son of Volok across the head with it. He staggers into a wall and the tube drops at our feet. That's all I need. I snatch up the tube and bolt through the cabin, my heart rabbiting in my chest. What next? What am I doing? I can't think. There's a snarl behind me, a scrabbling of claws against wood, and my body is screaming for survival as I run, run, run, bumping off walls and bursting out onto the aft deck . . .

Where the others are waiting for me.

They've clambered aboard and stand in a half-circle to greet me like a company of accursed knights, their boat a specter lurking in the swells beyond. Their eyes and fangs glitter in the stormlight.

Everything inside me quails.

*So this is the end.*

There's a step behind me, and I turn to find the Son of Volok looming over me. Hair disheveled. Incensed but smug.

He leans down. "You will pay for betraying our blood father."

Rain slashes at me, freezing me to the bone. Long taloned fingers enclose the drafting tube, try to pluck it from my grasp, and I jerk it back hard, chin lifted in defiance.

"Fuck you," I whisper.

The nosferatu smiles, eyes locked on mine . . . and pinches my face with cold claws.

I suck in a breath, paralyzed and lifted onto tiptoe. Dark amusement flickers in those pinprick eyes. Then that thing's face opens, its jaw hanging down to give egress to a pair of long white fangs.

The world funnels down to that gaping black mouth.

And a harpoon smashes through its chest, sucking it back. There, then gone. The drafting tube is ripped from my hand, and then the cultist is hanging impaled from the cabin wall like a broken toy, the drafting tube dangling from nerveless fingers.

I whirl. The half-circle of my executioners on the aft deck whirl. There's another shape looming out of the slashing rain. An enormous, tapered shadow against the fitful light. Gleaming, black, dreadful, dream.

Another boat.

And in the following illumination of lightning, I see who's standing at the bow like some figure out of legend. Eyes blazing and bare tattoos livid in the glare. Teeth clenched in righteous determination. Mane of hair blowing in the wind. A steel trident gripped in either hand.

Kaipo.

My Kaipo, come back for me.

He bellows, a war cry splitting the sky with its thunder. And then the *Kanaloa* is ramming into my yacht in an unholy screeching of metal and fiberglass that seems not of this world, and Kaipo Kalawai'a is leaping through the air with the prongs of his tridents flashing like death, and I have never felt such joy.

# TWENTY-TWO

Kaipo lands aboard the yacht like a god ascending to earth: with a boom that quakes the deck, accompanied by a crunch of bone as one of his tridents punches through a Son of Volok and flattens him at his feet. He lingers there, breathing hard, one knee bent and crouched over his fallen prey like some avenging sea titan. He's stripped to the waist, tatted muscles slick and brutal in the storm, silvery scars writhing over his body like glowworms, and his head stays bowed as four words growl out beyond the curtain of curls hiding his face: "Do. Not. Touch her."

The nosferatu shrink back from the quiet menace in that voice, glancing uneasily at each other, and I feel a strange flutter in my stomach.

Kaipo lifts his head, slits of white shining out through the tangles of his wet hair, and in the hard glint in his eyes I see the soldier he's always been . . . and something else.

I feel as if I've been touched by fire.

There's a shifting among the nosferatu, horny claws pushing out from their cuticles as they tense to strike, and Kaipo's nostrils flare as he whips his head. "Ilsa!" he roars and tosses me his free trident.

He doesn't wait for me to catch it. He's already moving, shrugging his remaining weapon free and swinging it in a vicious arc. Thick columnar arches of black blood rise like snakes and a body topples, its neck bubbling like a stew. Then something's bouncing across the deck and bumping against my ankle. A gaping face, fanged and hoar, its eyes aghast. A head.

I blink. There's a high-pitched ringing in my ears. Or maybe that's Kaipo, shouting my name again.

Because I have no time, either.

Claws sweep down at me, glinting in the rain, and without thinking I block them on the shaft of my trident. Sparks leap. The impact shudders down my arms into my bones, and for a moment they go numb. A nosferatu, pale and slender in the soaking rain, snarls at me and comes on. More blocks, more sparks as I'm driven back across the deck. Then I'm ducking another swipe of those claws and burying the tines of the trident into cold flesh, impaling the still, undead meat of the nosferatu's heart. A nasty thrill of triumph twists inside me as the cultist drops to his knees.

But there are more of them. Clambering over the rails, pulling themselves out of the seething waves, business suits soaked and cold eyes glittering. More of them than I can handle.

"With me!" Kaipo roars.

I leap to his side, and then we're back-to-back, legs planted wide on the pitching deck, tridents slashing and stabbing through the air. Even through my wetsuit, I can feel the heady, overwhelming warmth of his body, the strong beat of his heart—as familiar to me as the backs of my eyes—drumming against my ribcage. With every movement, I can feel the powerful twist of his back muscles, sense where he'll be next, and intuition takes over. Without a word, without planning it, we move as one, complementing and completing each other's movements. He sweeps wide to spin a cultist away and I duck under his scything swing to stab another approaching him from his left, switching places with him. I go low to take out a cultist's knees and Kaipo leaps over me to deliver a death blow to the chest. It's like dancing. Seamless, intimate, exhilarating. It's like making love.

And all the while, the words exult in my head: *He came back for me. He came back for me.*

At last, there's only one left. Kaipo claims him. He moves with a brutal efficiency that has a muscular grace to it, sidestepping an uppercut of talons and cracking the cultist's skull with the butt of his trident staff. Then he's pinning the Son of Volok to the deck with his foot, and with both hands he raises his three-pronged spear and drives it down with all his strength, steel tines biting through flesh to lodge deep in the deck beneath. He leaves the trident quivering upright in the air like a tuning fork and scans the storm, checking for the Sons of Volok boat. But it's gone. We've fought them off for now. We're safe.

Then he turns to me, breathing hard.

I don't think. I drop my trident with a clank at my feet and do what I've always wanted to do. I fling myself against the solid bulk of him, arms wrapping tight around him, my head tucked under his chin and our wet hair mingling together in the rain, goldish-brown and pale blond, as the deck shudders and the sea surges up in showers of spindrift on either side of us.

I breathe in his scent, that mix of sea brine, beard oil and man, and the boom of his heart against my breast feels like home.

"Kaipo," I whisper into him, everything I want to tell him jumbling together and clogging in my throat, and I don't know what I'll say next.

But he's gently pulling back so he can hold my face in his hands, dipping his head to look me in the eyes. "I should never have left you," he growls, making sure I hear the sincerity and self-recrimination in every word. "I was hurt. And I'll hurt far more when I lose you. But at least this way I can live with myself."

I let out a breath past the sting in my nose. "I don't know if I can bear hurting you again—"

He shakes his head, long lank locks plastered to his face, his kingly beard dripping rain. "I thought by leaving before you left me, I'd avoid feeling abandoned. But by leaving, I was really abandoning myself." He drops his head and lets out a shuddering breath, raises it again to show he's shut his eyes. He opens them, and they have never looked so bright. "Whatever comes—whatever I may go through—it will be worth it. To make you"—his throat bobs—"happy. And to have whatever time I get with you."

My stomach drops. Something in my battered chest melts. That sting in my nostrils reaches my eyes, and I lift a hand to lay it against Kaipo's wet cheek. He goes absolutely still under my touch, his eyes locking onto mine, and I know by the wild, careening feeling in my heart and the crackling charge in the air—the charge in that touch—that this moment has the kind of combustibility where anything can happen.

"Kaipo," I murmur, and swallow hard as he furrows his brow, straining with every muscle in his body to hear over the storm. "You should know that I—"

But the boat groans, veering alarmingly under our feet. I stagger and Kaipo catches me, glancing about at the veering deck. "She's sinking. The *Kanaloa* must've put a hole in her hull. We need to get out of here."

But I shake my head. "Not before I say this first." He turns to me, face softening as I struggle for words, afraid to let this moment go, afraid I'll never have it again. "I really need you to know that I—"

There's a blur, a crack and heavy thump, and then Kaipo is lying at my feet, blood matting his hair and creeping out from under his head onto the deck in a shiny crimson pool. He doesn't stir again.

I don't hear his heart.

I blink. It doesn't make sense. I look up, and the Son of Volok that had been impaled on the cabin wall is swaying before me in the rain, a gaping hole in his chest, the butt of the harpoon clutched in his hands dripping with Kaipo's blood.

Kaipo. He hit Kaipo. He caved his skull in.

He killed him.

A great roaring fills my ears.

"Traitors," the cultist spits, and then his head swivels fast enough to crack bone. The atlas. The drafting tube. It's sliding in the wash of water on the pitching deck, and with the roll of the waves, it skates aft—dangerously close to the edge.

I take no notice. Because Kaipo. Because—blood. Because—he's gone.

I'm alone again.

Alone. With nothing but my anger.

The harpoon clangs on teak. The cultist leaps for the atlas, but never gets there—because I've leapt to intercept him.

We collide midair in a sprawl of limbs and wash up hard against a fiberglass gunwale, the impact jolting through me as we're sucked back again. I don't feel anything through the rage flooding my veins. I'm numb, my vision stained red with vengeance. I slowly rise, taking my time. I have become an implacable, unstoppable force. The cultist, on the other hand, scrambles madly for the atlas, swiping for the strap of the drafting tube, but I drag him toward me with horrendous strength. "Stop!" he snarls, voice shrill with desperation. "We have to save it! It's the key to everything!"

But I'm not listening. I flip the cultist over and sit on him hard, knees straddling him, and slash with my own claws. Blood streaks the deck. The Son of Volok screams, but I don't see his face. I don't see anything resembling a man. All I see is something that took Kaipo from me. That opened up that howling void again. That needs to be destroyed.

"Listen to me!" the cultist begs. He tries to shield his face with his arms, and my claws tear them to shreds, leaving flesh hanging in strips. "You can't lose it either! You'll never find your husband without the atlas!"

I don't hear him. This reasoning doesn't register with me at all. Who is he referring to?

"Did you hear me?" the cultist shrieks. "You'll lose him forever!"

He swipes blindly above him with one hand, fingers grazing the drafting tube. It pinwheels on the teak and stops, half off the edge of the swim deck, teetering precariously on the brink. One rogue wave or dip of the boat and it'll be lost forever in the deep.

But I don't care.

I think of Kaipo falling. I think of his face. I think of losing him forever.

It injects me with fuel, overawing rage surging through me. I slash over and over, blood leaping from my claws. "You bastard," I croak, the words catching as sobs in my throat. "You filth. You coward. You took him from me. You *took him* from me!"

Eventually, the arms drop, and I'm slashing at the cultist's defenseless chest, neck, and face. He's not making any noises anymore. His body jostles with the blows, and I don't care where those blows land. I don't see much anymore; my eyes have filled up with tears, turning everything into a blur of salt and blood.

And I go on, and on, and on, that ever-present, bottomless anger in me cresting into a fury I can no longer contain and which leaves my lungs burning with raw, seething sobs.

And then, a hand on my shoulder. A gentle, firm grip. "Ilsa."

At first, I don't hear. Not through the choking sobs, the slowing, almost petulant swipes.

Then, firmer: "Ilsa."

The hand tugs at me, and I turn and blink up at him. Kaipo, standing over me, blood caking one side of his face and glistening in his golden-brown mane. His expression is almost sorrowful. "It's okay," he says. "I'm okay."

My brow furrows in confusion. "But—but you—"

"It's all right," he soothes, hunkering down to take my wrist. "You saved me. You can stop now."

I look down. I've turned the cultist into a horror of ravaged flesh. His face is unrecognizable, slashed to a raw pulp. His neck a ruin of tattered rents welling blood. His chest an ugly crosshatch of claw marks. I've desecrated him.

This is me. This is what my anger can do. This is what I carry inside me.

And Kaipo saw it all.

Shame and humiliation burn through me like wildfire. I can't look Kaipo in the eye, can't even glance in his direction. I stare down at my gore-slick hands, salt stinging the back of my throat, and wait for his judgment.

But he doesn't say anything. He leans to pick up the atlas, and when I look up, he's offering it to me, the wet plastic case gleaming with a sheen of absolution.

My heart twinges. Of course he's forgiven me. He knows who I am. He accepted everything about me the moment he saw me.

There's nothing I need hide from him.

Kaipo knits his brow, confused. So I rise, but I leave the atlas hanging in the air between us. Instead, I shuffle into his arms like a sniffling child waking from a nightmare.

Kaipo stills all over, the great sheets of muscle in his back tensing as I press myself against him. Then his arms wrap—tentative—around me, then more firmly. My shoulders heave.

"I know," he whispers, his breath warm on my scalp. "I know." He strokes my hair.

I draw in a long, shaky inhalation and let it out, my shoulders dropping as I think, *Home.*

And then the thing at our feet gives a wet gurgle.

We both look down at it. It's laughing, looking up at us from the ruin of its face with a smirk twisting its split lips. Kaipo's face hardens.

I take the atlas from him and kneel down to brandish it in the cultist's face. "Why were you after this?" My voice lowers. "Does it have to do with Arie?"

That smirk widens, lips splitting to ooze more blood.

My stomach clenches.

"It does, doesn't it?" I grip his shoulders and shake him. "Are you trying to end Arie's reign? Tell me!"

Kaipo holds me back. "Ilsa," he grits, glancing around at the sinking ship. "We should go—"

But I try to shrug him off, letting loose a string of vicious German—

And then the Son of Volok gurgles again, freezing me in place.

"Your bitch . . . Commodore . . . doesn't have long now." His smug laugh turns into a wretched cough that forces black blood like tar out of the rents in his neck. "She . . . will meet her end . . . He will make sure . . . of that . . ."

Ice infuses my veins. Kaipo and I exchange a look of horror.

"What do you mean?" Kaipo growls. "Who? Who will?"

And those gashed lips quiver up into an awful smile. "He is coming . . ."

His breath rattles wetly in his throat and releases in a final, pathetic sigh as his head falls back, his bloodshot eyes staring sightlessly up at the pouring rain.

I can't move. I feel as if my ribcage has been cracked open, my organs scooped out.

"Ilsa." Kaipo tugs my elbow again. "Come on!"

I look about. The sea is rushing up the deck toward us; the boat is slipping under the waves in a dreadful shuddering of wood and piping, tipping our side up into the air. I throw the drafting tube strap over my head, and then corpses are sliding into the water and I'm leaping at the last moment to grab Kaipo's hand, letting him help me clamber up onto the upended gunwale and then the bow of the *Kanaloa*. And we both look back, gripping the rail, and watch as that ill-starred yacht goes under in a hungry maelstrom of bubbles, drowning the slain Sons of Volok and what they've told me, the fact that is now blaring a warning inside my skull, over and over:

Arie's in trouble.

# TWENTY-THREE

Kaipo's wound isn't nearly as bad as I thought. Once the worst of the storm passes, I take him into the head and sit him on the toilet, apply hydrogen peroxide to the gash on his scalp. I know it must sting like hell, but he does not react at all, the weight of his eyes burning my face like a branding iron. I studiously avoid that gaze, not knowing what would happen if I meet it, feeling a subtle heat in my cheeks. So I busy myself with thread and needle, my stitches as neat as a welding line.

When I'm stowing the first aid kit back under the sink, he finally speaks.

"Ilsa."

I stiffen. The tenderness in that one word, as if my name were an invocation of salvation and suffering, makes my hands tremble.

"Ilsa. I need to ask you something."

*Please, don't ask that. Not now.*

But he does. "What were you going to tell me on that boat?"

*Shit.* I shut the cabinet door and stand so I can brace my hands on the sink, shoulders tensed, and study the woman staring back at me from the mirror. Is that the kind of woman who can give an honest answer in this moment? What would I think of that woman?

I turn around to face him, chin lifted like a scrappy street urchin's. "You want to know what I think?"

Wordlessly, he nods.

I lean down to say it into his face: "Fuck your family."

He blinks.

"That's right." I straighten so I can cross my arms over my chest. "Fuck 'em. Fuck your father, and fuck your mother and sisters for enabling him. Fuck 'em for abandoning you, and most of all fuck 'em for making you feel unlovable. Just because they can't see everything beautiful in you doesn't mean I can't. They don't know what they're missing out on."

My breathing is a little uneven by the time I'm done, my whole body shaking, and Kaipo is looking at me wide-eyed, a small grin playing about his lips, as if he's just witnessed someone mouth off in church. As if I've committed the ultimate sin: voicing the forbidden.

Voicing the truth.

I can't help it. He looks so vulnerable, so boyish and stripped of all armor sitting on that toilet in that cramped head, I uncross my arms so I can brush a gold-tinted lock of hair away from his lion's face. My fingers are trembling, my voice hushed. "You're an amazing man, Fishman."

Those deep brown eyes glass up, helplessly skittering away before finding mine again. And for a brief moment, they're not the eyes of a lion. They're the eyes of a puppy, dazzled and grateful. "Thank you," he gruffs, his chin trembling. "You're an amazing woman, Shipwright."

My heart clenches, and I feel something in me waver, something in the air between us draw tight as a mason line.

It only draws tighter when Kaipo smiles a sort of ironic, self-deprecating smile. "But that wasn't what you were going to say, was it?"

My spine stiffens. A tumult rises in my ears. All kinds of scary urges clamor inside me.

"No," I say at last, letting out a long sigh. "It wasn't."

He nods, groping for words. "Maybe it's not fair to ask, but . . ."

"Kaipo." I place a gentle hand on his shoulder, stopping him or steadying myself, I can't tell which. "Not now. Not yet."

He drops his head and nods again, ever the gentleman. He would never push me.

My heart somehow clenches even more, heavy with tenderness, and I squeeze. "We have to go. We know how to find the Hole of Souls now." I draw myself up, my whole body thrumming. "There's not a moment to lose."

Within minutes, we head for the Bay of the Dead.

I change out of the wetsuit and back into Kaipo's old clothes. The comforting feel of them on my skin is immediate. I stand there a moment, breathing in Kaipo's familiar scent, a great calm settling over me. Then I snap out of it and ascend to the wheelhouse.

While Kaipo's at the helm, scanning the predawn gloom for the Sons of Volok boat, I slide the atlas out of its tube and spread it out on the chart table. I need a distraction. For all of Kaipo's unquestioning acceptance, I still feel awkward around him, painfully conscious of the volcanic rage he saw in me. And I don't know how to be around him in this moment. He gives me a respectful distance, a lonely, wondering look behind his eyes, but does not press me. I'm grateful. Because I'm still trying to sort through my feelings of guilt and joy and heartache surrounding us.

So I focus on the atlas. I need answers.

The same old maps, the same old names. I try to look at them with fresh eyes: BLOODTOWN, THE GRAVEYARD OF LAIRS, THE FORGE OF THE BLOODSMITH. Possible clues in ornamental drawings, cryptic verso text. But nothing jumps out at me. Nothing rings a bell.

Eventually, I rub my eyes with a groan. "I don't understand. What in here could have anything to do with Arie?"

"We'll figure it out. Maybe you'll find more clues on our journey."

I frown. "Maybe." I turn a page. "But I feel like there's something in here staring me in the face."

Kaipo's beard twitches in a smile. "I have every confidence you'll put it together."

I give him a grateful look and set the page down. "I feel like I owe Arie something. And what if I can't warn her of what's coming in time? I don't know if I'd ever forgive myself."

Kaipo takes one big hand off the helm and wraps it around mine. My breath hitches at the touch. "We'll find it out together."

I look up into the calm reassurance in his eyes, the contact of our fingers sparking, sending warmth up my arm, into my chest and face. Then I slide my hand out of his and tear my eyes away before I don't have the strength to.

Kaipo swallows, a wounded look coming over his face, and stares out at the sea. I do not allow myself to think of how much this is hurting him. I do not dwell on how unfair this is. *He made his choice*, I remind myself. *He knew how things must go if he came back*. I want to do something, make some gesture to tell him how I feel. But I know it would be worse, far worse, if I let him in again.

I'm staring unseeingly at the atlas when Kaipo lifts a brow. "I think we're here."

I shoot him a glance, then rise from the chart table. While I'd been sitting there, the last of the night and the storm had melted away. The sea, blazing with sunlight, roils with fog steaming off the water. And when the tendrils of fog part, as if in invitation, a mangrove swamp shimmers into being like a mirage: The Bay of the Dead.

Gooseflesh ripples down my arms.

Kaipo juts his chin at the atlas. "The coordinates right?"

I flip pages until I find the right one, pointer finger checking latitude and longitude, and reference our chart plotter. I nod.

"Okay, then."

He kills our speed and turns our bow toward the swamp. There's an opening ahead, glimpsed through the drifts of fog, a still waterway looking much like the entrance to a maze. Kaipo glances over his shoulder, checking one last time to make sure we're not being followed, and glides us in.

It's a jungle. The water is a dark, murky green, stained by tannin from the leaves, and the gnarled mangrove roots stab down into the water like bundles of spears, forming winding corridors through the vegetation. Citing the map, I tell Kaipo which turns to take, guiding him in a spiral, closer and closer, toward the heart of the maze.

I don't know how long it takes. Ten minutes. Or an hour. The temperature warms, the air becoming humid. The seaweed brininess of the Red Sea fades away to be replaced by the rich tidal funk of sulfur and salt marshes. But at last the vegetation opens up again and the *Kanaloa* glides out onto a lake at the jungle's center, the sun beating off the water almost blinding us.

The first thing I see are the faces. They're gargantuan, hewn out of the living rock of the mountains on the far side of the lake. A pair of them looming like sphinxes above the writhing tendrils of fog, presiding in fierce and eternal dignity in the shadow of the sun. Their crowns carven with the headdresses of pharaohs. Their mouths bared to show huge fangs projecting down like pillars.

The watchers over the Bay of the Dead.

I shiver; I know what they're watching. For there, where the fog has been burned away, the water grows darker and darker, turning a blue so deep it's almost black. Kaipo kills the engine and we step out onto the gangway to look.

Below us, the shallow seabed drops away into a yawning hole of darkness big enough to swallow a fleet of yachts, its rim blurred by a sifting fog of sand like an exhalation from the depths. It looks like a portal to the underworld.

My stomach rolls over and I grab the rail, gripped by a sudden lurch of vertigo.

I have to go down into that.

I think of lying beneath the deep, the crushing weight of oceans in my lungs, and fight down a wave of nausea.

Kaipo is watching me, but I can't meet his eyes. Not now. That would be too much vulnerability.

The fisherman lazily pulls his eyes away from me and studies the blue hole again. "Quite a place to imprison someone." He scans those fanged colossi carved into rock. Perhaps wondering, as I am, whose likenesses they capture, and who carved them. "Volok must have really hated this blood son of his."

"He loved him, actually."

"Really?" Kaipo rocks his head in place, impressed. "Didn't know the old fiend had it in him." I feel those eyes on me again, warming my skin. "What did he do?"

"The blood son?" I shrug, fending off a shiver. "Don't know the details; I was stuck on Transmarinia for most of it. All I know is he rallied a number of their yachting club and tried to overthrow him."

Kaipo's eyebrows climb into his hairline. "Sounds like a badass, if you ask me."

I snort, but any humor soon fades as I gaze down into that blue hole again. Kaipo clocks this, and with an air of breezy enthusiasm he claps his hands, the echo of it rebounding off the giant stone visages and back across the lake to us. "Ready to dive into some graves?"

Before I can fetch my wetsuit, he finds one for me. A black full-body vulcanized rubber looking like a shed skin. I take it and lift a brow.

Kaipo flushes. "Oh. Right."

He turns around while I strip and step into the wetsuit, making sure I stay in the shade of the fishing arch and out of the sun. The neoprene grips my skin like the suckers of a squid, molding to my curves. It's faded by sun and scraped by coral, clearly well-worn. Clearly a woman's suit. I wonder how many other women have worn this, if there's been a parade of liveaboard girl toys and I'm just the latest. A nasty little hook of jealousy I have no right to feel catches in my stomach and pulls, unraveling the ugly mix of emotions inside me.

"Ilsa?" He's still standing with his back to me like a gentleman, hands clasped before him.

"Mm?"

He looks down at his bare feet, as if considering how to say what follows. "I know you're scared."

I can't help but scoff. "Scared?" I pull the silvery sleekness of my hair out of the suit and let it dangle down my back. "I'm not scared."

"No? Because it's okay if you are."

I shake my head and grip the zipper on the front of the suit, begin to race it up my midline. "Why would I be scared to go down there—"

"Because it reminds you of your slumber beneath the sea."

The zipper halts halfway up my front.

"Arie told me. She said you were down there for a long time while you were healing." He turns and pales, his eyes going round at my zipper halted right under my pushed-together cleavage. There's a booming in my ears, a strange tingle between my thighs, and I zip it all the way up.

He snaps his eyes up and swallows. "That must have been terrible for you."

I grasp onto lovely, faithful anger amid a sudden rush of dizziness at his eyes on me. "Why would it have been—"

"Because it made you feel trapped. Powerless. In the same way you were powerless when Volok had you enslaved all those years on that island."

I swallow hard, feeling suddenly naked and exposed.

"That's right. I know you, Ilsa." He lets out a marveling whoosh of air. "I know so much about you it scares me."

My eyelid twitches. I feel a dangerous blooming in my chest, like a lotus unfurling to expose its delicate heart. I try to squash it.

"Kaipo," I barely whisper. "Stop."

But he won't be stopped now. He takes a careful step toward me, his shaggy lion's face aching. "I know you've hidden yourself for centuries, thinking you don't deserve to be seen by anyone."

I take a step back, try to shake my head. To shake away what he's saying.

"But it's impossible not to see you, Ilsa Knackenkusser. I know you've cut yourself off from everything. I know you've devoted your entire life to others—to the women on Transmarinia, to Arie, to her quest—because you don't think you're deserving of the same sacrifice. Because you believe you've failed your husband. Or maybe, deep down, you believe that if he loved you enough, he would have found a way to come back to you. So maybe you're not worth it if he hasn't."

"Stop," I whisper. I'm begging now, my voice shaking. How can it be this wonderful to be seen like this? How can it be so terrible?

But he goes on.

"I know you're a fighter. I know why you lose yourself in your work. I know that you feel like your life was smashed into a million pieces, and that if you just focus hard enough you can somehow weld it back together, like one of your boats. And you do that through the sheer force of your rage—"

*"Stop, goddamn you!"* I put my hands over my face, lungs hitching and wanting to hide, wanting to disappear into that cresting wave of shame. But Kaipo grabs my wrists and gently pulls them away.

"Hey," he says. "I get it. I get it more than anyone else could. You're terrified your anger scared me off? It didn't. I'm right here."

I hiccup a sob and blink at him through glistening eyes.

His face gentles and he cups my chin with thumb and forefinger. "You think I don't know anything about that kind of abandonment? That feeling of worthlessness? That rage at all the wrong in the world?" He shakes his head in wonderment. "I know, Ilsa. I know."

My eyes dart back and forth as I stare into that sympathetic face. The kindness there makes my bottom lip quiver. I hate myself for it and still it with a bite of my teeth, feeling a roil of guilt for not believing he'd understand. *But you don't know*, I silently scream, wanting to be heard. *You don't know*. The backs of my eyes burn, scalded with unshed tears, but I refuse to cry. "I watched him," I whisper, feeling the need to explain, to defend my rage on that boat. "Do you understand? I watched Volok take my love from me. I watched him take my *life* from me. Do you know what it feels like to be imprisoned on an island for *centuries*? To labor for your oppressor, delivering him the means of enslaving others, while every day not knowing if your love is still alive?

To be unable to sleep because you can't stop thinking about all the ways you want to unmake him? To have that vengeance poison your heart over the long years until all that's left is rage?"

My voice is rising, getting away from me, but I don't care. Kaipo is watching me, a tender look of sadness in his eyes, but also satisfaction. Like an oilman finding a gusher in the desert.

It drives me over the edge.

"You think you understand my anger? You think you understand the kind of rage that will keep you going for centuries?" I stab him in the chest with a finger. "I guarantee you have no fucking idea."

After a long, fraught silence filled with my heavy breathing, he parts his lips. "And does that anger feel good?"

My insides drop. Shame and a strange twinge of humiliation floods my face.

But I lift my chin. "It doesn't have to. That's not what it's for."

Kaipo shakes his head, an almost pitying look in his eyes. "You think it'll get you through anything. It won't. Anger can be helpful. It can even be what saves you. But it's never what brings you peace."

I cross my arms and look away, nostrils flared and feeling cornered. I don't like the direction this conversation has taken. "Where's the diving caddy—"

But Kaipo is shaking his head. "I think you should freedive."

I can't help it: My jaw drops. *"What?"*

He shrugs. "You don't need a suit down there. You don't need to breathe, and there's no chance of the cultists finding us here." He gestures to take in the steaming mass of mangroves around us. "We're hidden."

"Then why don't you—"

"I think it's important you do this on your own."

I chew on my bottom lip, wanting to make an excuse—to say something sharp—but holding it in.

He seems to know exactly what's going through me. His mouth quirks up one side and he runs his hands up and down my arms, setting off sparks and chills all over my body. His voice a gentle rumble. "Just try."

"Once I find him," I whisper, sounding more childish than I'd like. "Once I find my husband, I'll be whole again. That anger will go away."

He holds my gaze, that deep brown seeming to go on forever. "And if it doesn't?"

I look away. I don't want to think about that.

His hands move again, up and down my arms, bringing out goose bumps all along my skin inside the wetsuit. "Try. For me. Try to feel what I feel when I'm down there. Try to let it go."

I look up at him, eyes welling, the raw hope in my heart almost embarrassing. "What do you see?"

That mysterious quirk in his mouth comes back, twitching his lion's beard. "You'll know when you feel it."

I stare into those smiling eyes, that boundless humor of his infectious, irresistible. I feel a great sliding within myself, a responding leaping of joy, and am suddenly aware that it wouldn't take much to lean forward and melt into him. His hands, on my arms, gently grip me, thumbs brushing back and forth. Daring. Testing. And I don't move away. I sway back and forth, ever so slightly, with every brush of his thumbs, in rhythm with his body. Touches and allowances. Risks and permission.

His eyes drop to my lips, back up to my eyes. His own lips part.

I think of his voice when I drank from him. I think of him calling my name.

I think of doing that again.

A pulse quivers in his right dimple, and I wonder what it would be like to bite his lips, feel them burst hot and scarlet in my mouth.

I take a shaky but resolute step back. "I should go."

Kaipo blinks; the spell is broken. He rubs the back of his neck. "Right." He rummages a weight belt out of the diving caddy, clips something onto it and hands it to me. I place it around my waist with the weights resting at my hips and snap it tight. Then he's pulling fins onto my feet with the care of a prince fitting me with glass slippers, and my throat narrows. *I don't deserve this gentle giant. I would only ruin him.*

He hands me a flashlight and a pair of bolt cutters, steps back and opens his mouth, hesitates, and says, "Good luck."

But I hear what he wanted to say, all the same: *I wish we didn't meet like this.*

My lip trembles. *Me, too.*

Then I'm leaping into a back dive off the *Kanaloa*, and Kaipo's aching face is whirling away from me and all is a blur of blue sky and clouds and undead giants carved into rock, and then darkness is swallowing me and all thoughts of Kaipo are dashed away as I plunge headfirst into the Hole of Souls.

# TWENTY-FOUR

It's nothing but darkness.

At first, there's blue, dark but there. Then the bouquet of bubbles clears and I find myself suspended over a gaping maw of an abyss that is as black and frigid as space. Around me, sunlight pierces down from above, penetrating that darkness in vertical shafts. But they only go so far. It is a sinkhole of blackest madness.

Terror fills me, a screaming, thalassophobic panic. The memory of being trapped below the sea rushes down my throat and fills my lungs. The memory of rats suffocating me. My old mortal instincts kick in and I convulse, waiting to drown. Bubbles stream from my open mouth. I shut my eyes. And I wait it out. I think of Reinhard's (*Kaipo's*) smile. I think of Reinhard's (*Kaipo's*) arms around me. I think of thumbs gently brushing my arms, back and forth, calming me.

*(Try. For me.)*

I open my eyes.

I'm still floating above the blue hole, sand sifting down from its rim into the black like underwater waterfalls. I breathe in water, let it fill me, and taking the flashlight dangling from my wrist, I click it on.

A beam of light blazes downward, failing to reach the bottom. I waggle my fins and follow it.

It's not dead down here. There are growths on the limestone walls of the sinkhole, on the fang-like stalactites of its overhangs. They bristle with pink algae, red sponges, brown moss and the shells of mollusks. And the darkness is not still—fish dart by, striped with color. Parrotfish. Groupers. Blunt-nosed reef sharks prowling a gloom floating with a fluffy marine snow of plankton filaments and husked shells. It's stunning, the stark purity of it a devastation of beauty. I sense an understanding of what Kaipo sees in it stirring within me, almost within reach.

But then I hit a halocline, the water growing so cold it'd take the breath from me if I *were* breathing. And all life dies.

It's not just the cold—there's something else lurking under the halocline. I taste it on my tongue. Sulfur. There's a layer of sulfur hanging below me. It turns the world green, plunging the chasm into clouds of deadly gas that have settled on the bottom like an eerie, restless mist, shrouding everything.

Or almost everything.

For something rises out of that mist. It's in the center of the hole's floor, where the debris of centuries has accumulated to form a barrow-mound of sorts. It's littered with bones: the spines of fish, the jaws of antediluvian sharks, the great grinning skull of some leviathan as if this were the lair of some prehistoric mastodon. But as the beam of my flashlight crawls over them, I find that that's not all. There are mummies down here, frightful figures wrapped in linen cloth and preserved by the gases since the days of the pharaohs, their arms crossed and gums retreated to bare rows of fluted teeth in slack jaws. And embedded upright in that mound, leaning here and there like tombstones in the shifting clouds of sulfur as if they had been carelessly dumped there from above, are a collection of iron coffins.

Goosepimples ripple down my body.

So the stories are true. Volok, back in the day, had a blood son who rebelled against him.

And he's here somewhere.

I kick down, my fins scattering gas into wisps of green smoke as I float closer. The iron of the coffins is scaled with rust, pitted and porous with corrosion from the hydrogen sulfide. Still, you can see how beautiful they must have been once. Hammered into harsh, gothic designs carved with wolf's-head handles and ornate runes and a chilling heraldry of the undead. All of them, to a one, wrapped in heavy links of chain so whatever is within can't escape without.

And near the top of every coffin, where the head of the body would be, gape small windows encaged in a grill of bars.

My hand is shaking when I sweep my flashlight over the windows.

In every one, pairs of watching eyes glow back at me like pinpricks of ice.

Somehow, here in the cold deep, I grow colder.

*You're safe*, I remind myself, hefting the bolt cutters. *They can't touch you.*

Now to find him.

I make a slow circuit before the coffins, peering into the windows with my torch. The eyes retreat, squinting against the light, and I glimpse faces hanging in putrescent runs and tatters. I wonder if I'll recognize him after so many years. If he'll have changed down here due to the slow insult of decay.

Eventually, I'm left with a final coffin standing alone in the center. The coffin is engraved with pentacles, heptagrams, occult runes and sigils, as if sorcery as well as iron were necessary to imprison the being within. Then the beam of my flashlight snags on a V and I freeze.

V for Volok. The signet of his blood son.

My beam travels up to the window of the coffin.

I see the eyes first, glowing like witchfire before revealing themselves to be pale and cloudy, the corneas seeming to float loose on the whites, giving them a slightly deranged look. Then I see it, framed by long fine black hair floating like seaweed in tide. His face.

Even with my lungs filled with water, I feel the impulse to swallow.

I lean the bolt cutters against the coffin and unzip a bag on my weight belt, take out the dive slate there. It's a white rectangle of plastic with a graphite pencil hooked to it. I unhook the pencil and scribble, hold the slate up to the window.

A pair of rotting hands grip the iron bars, dislodging motes of rust, and the blood son of Volok squints to read the words: REMEMBER ME?

Those unsettling eyes lift to my face, and the blood son nods.

I rub out the words with my wrist and scribble another message, hold up the slate again: WHERE'S MY HUSBAND?

The blood son's answer is to reach a hand through the bars. Gray-green, mottled with mold, long nails grown into talons as the cuticles have retreated, crusted with fungus tinged a gangrenous shade.

I try not to touch him as I hand him the pencil, hold the slate for him while he scrawls with laborious slowness. I can see the tendons showing through his decayed knuckles, moving like puppet-strings.

When he's done, I turn the slate toward me and shine the flashlight on it.

WHY WOULD I TELL YOU?

A hard, small anger coils in my stomach, and I wipe away what he wrote and replace it with my message, hold it up to him: BECAUSE I'LL FREE YOU IF YOU DO.

And I lift up the bolt cutters so he can see them.

Those cloudy eyes fixate on the cutters, then on my face. As if wrestling with old resentments, old hatreds.

He offers his rotting hand.

It does not take him long. He writes only one word: TRANSMARINIA.

He watches my face as I read. What he sees there makes him grin, a crescent gnarling of teeth glaring sickly at me through a hole in his cheek.

I feel strange and faint as I write: WHERE?

His answer: CAVE AT NORTH POINT.

His jaw is hanging down now, raw tendons moving like terrible straps, green-tinged fangs gleaming. He's laughing.

I suppose it is funny. It's a joke. A terrible joke that's been played on me.

My husband. Reinhard. He was there on Transmarinia, all that time I was imprisoned there.

What cruelty.

I feel nauseous. I feel like I might throw up, if such a thing is possible down here.

Something slimy touches me, and I recoil as Volok's blood son takes the slate and pencil from me, scribbles a message and shows it to me: YOUR TURN.

His eyes are burning now, frightful with humor and expectancy. He is filled with a renewed vigor.

So I do what I promised. I stow the diving slate again and heft the bolt cutters, fit them to the chain-links binding the coffin and bear down hard. The blades bite through as if the iron were made of cookie dough, and the chains slide away in a whiffling of sulfur as I scramble backward, my heart thudding in my chest.

The coffin lid creaks open.

For a moment, the blood son lingers in that iron darkness. Then he peeks out into the faint light from above and shuts his eyes, the wrinkles in his face softening. He is clothed in a seaman's attire, ankle boots and a striped cotton shirt and canvas pants, ragged and stained a slimy black by sulfur. Underneath, he is a putrid, tattered corpse with slashes of skeleton showing through.

He meets my eyes and marches straight for me across the floor of the blue hole.

My heart shrivels. I scramble back and fall, bumping along the sinkhole floor, fins kicking up bones and shreds of greenish smoke as I struggle up again and brandish the bolt cutters, ready to fight off the bite of those moldering fangs.

But the blood son is indomitable. With alarming strength he snatches the bolt cutters out of my grasp, and bubbles rush out with my silent scream.

*No.* How could I be such a fool? How could I make the mistake of trusting him?

Unthinkingly, one word comes to my lips: *Kaipo* . . .

But the blood son marches right past me and cuts the chains of another coffin, wrenches it open.

Before I can recover, the blood son is embracing another coffin-dweller. Another man. Dark-skinned, with long dreads and a captain's tarred frock coat. Perhaps from the Caribbean.

They're lovers.

Then they've released another man from his coffin. Another seaman, sandy-haired, in the same striped shirt and canvas pants as the blood son. And all three of them are pressing their brows together with a tenderness that brings a lump to my throat.

Something is tugging at me. A faint pity, a twinge of recognition.

They were trapped down here, just like I was in my submarine slumber. Or my sentence on Transmarinia.

And they made it through. Their love got them through it.

They found love again.

I look away. I feel like this moment is too private—too intimate—to be witnessed.

I pick up the bolt cutters left forgotten in the ground-mist of sulfur and go to work.

It doesn't take long to free the others from their coffin-prisons. They drift out in wonder, hair afloat, eyes glowing, all sinew and rags of moldered flesh stretched tight over bone. They look up at the dappled furnace of the sun above, faces filled with yearning, and push off from the sinkhole bottom and up toward the light.

At the surface, it doesn't take them long to burst into flame. There's no agony in it. No torment. No struggle to save themselves. They have become bonfires of glorious release, like offerings to the eternal.

They're finally free.

Then the blood son and his lovers are looking at me. They all raise a hand in farewell and thanks, and I feel a stinging in my nostrils, a burning behind my eyes as I raise my hand in answer.

They kick off, green murk parting around them, bits of sailcloth and decaying flesh trailing after. And as those lovers swim up together, hands held and ready to meet their fate, I feel a great loosening around my heart, a sort of pulsing pang that's like the burning return of warmth after frostbite. Both a letting go and a remembering. An unburdening of the soul. An extraction of that ugly venom coursing through me, leaving my veins cool and humming with peace. If I could breathe, I'd be gasping.

And as I watch those lovers become flame and ash on the surface, my eyes blurring up, I think, *I understand now, Kaipo. I understand.*

*It's beautiful.*

# TWENTY-FIVE

When I surface in the safety of the *Kanaloa*'s shadow, Kaipo is waiting for me.

"Thank God," he whispers, his face white as I hand him my fins, bolt cutters, weight belt. "They all came up, and when they started burning, I thought—I thought—"

But I don't let him finish. As soon as I'm standing, I'm wrapping my arms around him, my head tucked under his chin, breathing in his comforting scent. "Thank you," I whisper.

At first, I think he'll say something. Make one of his jokes, or ask what the hell is going on.

But he doesn't.

Instead, he merely accepts the embrace and scoops me to him, drops his nose into my hair and breathes in, as if soaking up the luckiness of this moment.

We set course for Transmarinia.

It should take us two weeks to make the passage through the Suez Canal, across the Mediterranean and up the eastern coastline of Europe to Germany. It's slow hitting me. At long last, I know where my husband is. I know how to get to him. And it will only take a couple short weeks.

I should be ecstatic, I know. I should be overflowing with excitement at the prospect of seeing him again. But now that the moment is finally near, I find that a slow feeling of dread has sunk in, twisting at my insides.

So I decide to push it all away and not think about it.

As if by unspoken agreement, Kaipo and I carefully avoid any mention of our purpose, lapsing instead into a fantasy. At night we dock and spend hours wandering the dusty alleys of Egyptian villages, inspecting the colorful wares of the night bazaars and shouting over the shrieks of children as they ply us with beads and scarves and plaster scarab beetles. I watch Kaipo interact with them, delighting them with stories and then shooing them off to gales of laughter. I can't help but smile.

"How do you do it?" I finally ask.

He gives me a questioning look.

"How did you learn to be funny after"—I wave a hand—"everything."

He thinks on it a moment, ducking under a colorful canopy of rugs leaning out of a shopfront. "I learned to stop trying to control everything. Nothing can be funny if you're worried about the outcome."

More children find us, a riffraff in gaily colored rags trailing us through the mud brick arcades, around droves of camels with eyes clustered with flies. We wade through them undisturbed, shoulders touching as we point out wares, our hands occasionally brushing each other and lingering before separating again. We bring each other up-to-date on our lives. He tells me of life in the Navy and—briefly—as a mercenary, and I tell him of life on Transmarinia and how I helped Arie. I've never been so free with another person, and I do not question this abrupt departure from my old self. We pour out our stories with ironical remarks, somber passages, buoyant sympathy. Little by little, Kaipo coaxes a certain lightheartedness out of me. We laugh as if it is a game. As if the feelings that follow are a game. It's this quest, we're caught in a dream, this play-act is allowing us to be something we've never before imagined: carefree, without a future, in freedom and glorying celebration of life.

On our final night in Egypt, we drift by a shipyard where workers in helmets and sweat-stained shirts weld out hulls in sprays of sparks. Kaipo catches me watching. "What was Ilsa Knackenkusser like?" he asks. "Before she became a shipwright."

*More innocent, that's for sure.* "I don't know if you'd believe it if you heard it."

The depths of Kaipo's eyes glint. "Really? Now you have to tell me."

I shake my head, holding back a smile. "She was a little naïve, I'm afraid."

"Ah." Kaipo muses on this as we skirt the firefly sparks of the shipyard. "I think I'd rather enjoy meeting that Ilsa Knackenkusser."

"I bet you would," I mutter, the corners of my lips curling.

Kaipo places a hand on his chest in mock offense. "I'm rather offended by that implication." His face grows solemn as we walk on, his voice lower. "No. I'd just like to see you smile more."

My heart does something funny in my chest. "I think I've smiled more around you than I ever have in my life."

He gives me an inscrutable sidelong glance. "My sincerest apologies."

"Accepted. But don't let it happen again. Can't have you ruining my imposing German demeanor."

Kaipo stops in his tracks, taking me by the elbow. "Ilsa?"

I lift a brow, my heart pitter-pattering in my chest. "Yes?"

His face shines with something much like triumph. "I do believe you just told a joke."

Oh.

I blink at him, feeling rather flustered. "I did, didn't I?"

Kaipo grins ear to ear, his beard shining in the fitful light of the shipyard. He has never looked more handsome.

We transit the canal and cross the Mediterranean, heading out into the cold Atlantic. At first, we keep a sharp lookout for the Sons of Volok. But despite ourselves, our attentiveness becomes lazy, leisurely, the fraught tension of the first half of our trip giving way to a feeling of a couple on holiday, or a honeymoon. We glide through a charade of domesticity with a feeling of immense security—a security we have never felt in any of the places we've been before, places which should have had more of a claim of belonging on us. It's all a lark, and our happiness will last us for whatever the time required. We will never run out of things to tell each other.

But it does end. Much, much too quickly, the two weeks pass, and on the afternoon before arriving at Transmarinia, I wake from my daytime slumber and head abovedeck to find Kaipo.

I half expect him to be gone. He's been spearfishing a lot lately, diving while I sleep to return with the shimmering bodies of pike and herring shish-kabobbed on his spear. But he's not gone. There's a creaking of wood, and I follow it to find Kaipo clipped into a harness in his fighting chair, feet braced on the paddle, gripping a fishing rod set into a holder between his legs. The reel bows into an almost impossible arch from the strain, and Kaipo grips it with both hands, cursing under his breath. He hauls back on it, rocking back and forth, one hand whipping the crank when there's slack in the line, the muscles in his forearms striating in the sun. "Come on," he grunts, his hand a blur. The fishing line sings, a fragile tracery of silver in the sunlight, and then Kaipo is reeling in a brilliant sparkling of rainbow scales: a salmon. It's huge.

He swings it aboard with the jubilance of a schoolboy. "Oh, look at you," he coos. "You're a beauty." He catches me watching him with my arms crossed and leaning against the doorway and grins. "Hey. What's up?"

But I only smile and jut my chin. "Put that on ice."

His brows bounce up. "Why?"

I look at him boldface. "Because I want to freedive with you."

And his whole face glows.

The Baltic Sea is shockingly cold, so Kaipo opts for a drysuit, an old Seaskin scuffed with abrasions that makes him looked sheathed in armor. I stick with my wetsuit—I don't need the warmth, but it protects my skin from the sharp edges of rock and coral. The sun has dropped into the sea by the time we pull our fins on, and Kaipo hands me a flashlight, hooking its tether around my wrist. He smiles at me as we slip into the water and hang onto the boat. Then he goes away somewhere as he prepares himself. He's present, but not. It's as if he's entered a waking trance. That achingly familiar booming of his heart slows. His jaw slackens. His eyes hood down to half-mast. He takes deep, drowsy breaths, in and out, his enormous lungs working like a smithy's bellows. And now I know why he's so barrel-chested. It's not just the muscles: Over the years he's expanded his rib cage, developing its flexibility to increase his lungs' capacity to hold air. He sucks in one big inhalation, and then begins to take little sips of air that he compacts into his already full lungs. He's packing in every bit of oxygen he can for the dive ahead.

Then he gives me a nod, rolls over in a dolphin dive, and we're under.

It's a twilight world down there. For a few moments, the deep is a dim green the color of algae, the seabed below waving with meadows of seagrass. Then before our eyes the last of the day's afterglow fades away and we're plunged into darkness. The beams of our flashlights cut through the murk. Kaipo points his at himself, flashes me the okay sign and I sign back. He nods, his mane of hair a rippling sleekness behind him, and dives farther down.

The silence is absolute, pressing against our eardrums and achingly cold. Or almost absolute. Beside me the calm, steady boomings of Kaipo's heart, blipping out around us like sonar waves. He pinches his nose and blows, equalizing, and lifts his flashlight. Our beams give shape to a spooky marinescape of undulating meadows of bladderwrack, crabs scuttling across algae-mossed boulders. Here and there old shipwrecks hove out of the gloom like submarine specters, eerily preserved in the cold brackish waters of the Baltic: Swedish warships ranged with cannon, windjammers still strung with rigging and ghostly tatters of sail. We are steeped in the past.

Except we're not. As I float through an old German schooner, the beam of my flashlight flickering through its staves and swaying forests of kelp, I look over at Kaipo and realize that for him all sense of time has vanished. Down here where death is one breath away, there is no room for either the past or the future, because neither exist. There is no rumination. No thoughts of ostracism and estranged families. No worries of what the days ahead may bring. In his eyes, there is only the now. Only the here. Only life.

But it's more than that. It's all connected. Infinity in the miniscule. Shimmering solar nebulae in the iridescent umbrella of jellyfish. Black holes in a giant squid's eyeball. Baby chub in sea urchins. The wrinkles of old lovers in the sprawl of starfish.

Sons. Fathers. Love. Hate. Bitterness. Anger. Guilt. Shame. Despair. Death. Rebirth.

Down here, Kaipo found everything. Down here, Kaipo found life again.

Down here, he found his family.

I follow his gaze with new eyes, drink in the waving kelp and eelgrass, the looming walls of an underwater canyon. Clinging to it all a silence that now feels holy. A peace that is prevailing. That sense, again, of the eternal.

I smile.

Maybe I can find the same here. Maybe I can be freed.

When my flashlight traces those canyon walls again, however, they're higher now and curving overhead like hull panels. Maybe we've floated into the belly of a shipwreck. Or a whale. Some sort of mythical passage, a hallucinatory crossing. But no—I recognize this place. The arching beams above are not cetacean ribs but the rafters of a clubhouse I was forced to build long ago.

Somehow, we've floated into the Nosferyachtu Club down here.

The back of my neck goes crawly and strange.

It's been transformed. Sunken, ruined, the triangular club burgees hanging from the ceiling above slimed with something that glows with a ghastly green effulgence. They're all emblazoned with a jagged V.

A hum of dark expectancy fills me. I know what will be at the far end of the room. As I float toward it, I lift the beam of my flashlight.

The throne is still huge, still spiky, hewn from what looks like a hunk of driftwood riddled with shipworm and growths of coral and sponges. Enormous tentacles bulge and curl about it in languid shuttlings of protuberant sucker mouths. And a figure sits upon it.

My skin contracts.

The figure hunches in its seat, draped in seaweed and seemingly asleep. Conch shells and starfish and barnacles like nests of teeth encrust the pale flesh of its bald head, its icicle-like hands. It has a feeble chin and overbite, and a pair of fangs protrude down like those of a rat.

Then its eyes open, twin baleful moons, and former Commodore Volok looks at me.

Dread tolls in me like a bell.

In a crackling of barnacle bark and stirring of silt, the old fiend rises from his throne, trailing a cape of seaweed, his toothsome mouth swelling in a smug smile. A smile that brings back fangs sinking into a neck, and hot blood, and the screams of lovers torn apart. Of the clink of shackles and vengeance denied for centuries.

Goose bumps ripple down my back.

Volok takes a step down from his dais, his footfall echoing in the clubhouse.

*DOOM*

The smile swells.

*DOOM*

His icicle fingers unbutton his rotting frock coat, pull it wide to bare his breast.

*DOOM*

Another step and he's before me now, offering a cold dagger with a handle inscribed with occult runes. A sacrificial weapon.

He's offering himself to me. At long, long last, my moment of retribution.

Everything stills.

But I don't feel what I've always felt. I'm not overcome with rage, and grief, or even a bewildering loss that I can't avenge myself on him.

No. I observe that hideous face with the calm distance of a stranger.

That anger . . . it's gone.

I'm free.

The shambling marine horror takes one final step. The handle is right there. Even now, I could still take it—

*DOOM*

And I lift my eyes and think: *Thank you, anger. Thank you for protecting me. But I don't need you anymore.*

Volok freezes.

It happens immediately, as if a spell has been broken. As I watch, that figure crumbles. That face cracks and fragments, shattering like pottery. The lower jaw splits off, the head drops forward. All of it collapses in on itself in a mushroom cloud of chalk-white dust. And then the world comes apart. The clubhouse crumbles, the great slabs of hull panels groan and tumble down in low, thunderous booms and billowings of silt, shaking the ground beneath me. An underwater cataclysm. A majestic toppling of illusion.

And then it's just the canyon again. And I'm still here. Still me. That long slash Volok carved into my heart gone.

A hand slips into mine, our skin shimmering at the touch, and I'm brought back. Kaipo is looking at me, and I instantly know he knows what has just transpired inside me. His lips twitch in a smile, the skin wrinkling around his eyes, and I'm engulfed in a wave of throat-narrowing gratitude for him. For what he has shared with me and made possible.

We both rest our fins on the sand of the seabed, our flashlights dangling from our wrists in a soft sulfurous glow as we hold each other's hands down there in the dark, and rest our brows together. Our hair adrift, our eyes shut. Our spirits hushed and dizzy with wholeness.

# TWENTY-SIX

I'm not sure how long we've been down there by the time we surface. It feels like a lifetime, an eternity. But probably only five or six minutes. Champion freediving time for Kaipo. He places a hand on my shoulder and the air rushes from his body in an explosive gasp. Then he's filling his lungs with fresh air in steady, forceful draws, his eyes shut, his expression almost pained. He looks woozy, disoriented. Memories of him blacking out hit me and I hold him with one hand on his chest, soft with motherly care. I force away stories of freedivers coughing up blood. Getting the bends. Gas embolism. Seizure. Heart attack. Blood clots. Even—on rare occasions—dying.

No. I can't think that.

He's all right. He has to be all right.

I help him splash to the swim deck, guide him up the short steel ladder hanging off the side and make him sit on the teak boards we renovated with our own hands, his elbows on his knees, his magnificent head down. I sit beside him and towel his hair, press a cool water bottle to the back of his neck. I am melting, turning into a puddle of tenderness I have never known before. When he's ready to stand, I unzip his drysuit, tug it down his body as he stands there like a child, tousled and crusted with crystals of salt, one hand steadying himself on the fighting chair. Watching me. A small smile crooks his lips, and I feel my cheeks burn. I won't look at him, though. I can't look at him with these thoughts in my head. They're finally coming now, as if bursting through a crack in a hull I've been desperately patching up this whole time, trying to ignore. This man—he's put himself through hell to be with me. He put off his retirement. He risked his ship. His life. He's fought undead frights and abandonment terror and came back to help me finish this journey, even though he'd lose me in the end. And knowing all that, he did it anyway.

Who does that?

Not a man who doesn't care about you. Not a man who merely likes you.

Not a man who doesn't love you.

And this will be the final night I have with him. After tomorrow, that might be it. I may never see him again.

I'm suddenly dizzy. I can't stand straight. I kneel, knees shaking, and Kaipo watches me as I tug the drysuit off his legs. But when it's off, I don't stand. I bunch that damp skin into a ball and hold it to my chest, my eyes distant.

Kaipo's brows knit as he squints down at me. "You okay?"

*Yes*, I think. *Kneeling is right. Take a moment here. This is serious.*

The deck suddenly feels unstable beneath me. Untrustworthy. As if it were a trapdoor, ready to plunge me into some shadowy catastrophe or lifelong mistake. This is how it feels. This is how it always feels, when you are on the verge of changing who you are.

I stand, the rubber suit sliding from my hands. I meet Kaipo's eyes.

Then I push him back into the fighting chair and he lands in it in a creak of aged wood. His eyebrows shoot up in surprise, questioning. His bare chest rises and falls, the pretty shelves of his abs sucking in and out in bewilderment.

I decide to show him my answer, his gaze gluing to my hand as I finger the zipper of my wetsuit, pull it down in a sensuous purr of metal teeth. His eyes widen when he realizes I'm not wearing anything under the suit.

He drags himself up higher in the chair, his face whitening. "What—what are you doing?"

I don't respond. I keep my eyes on him as I pull down and down, revealing a long slash of bare skin to my belly button. His eyes flick up to mine, back down to my body, his breath held as if breathing would break the spell of what's transpiring here. I grasp the collar of my wetsuit and freeze. A silent communication, a language of pauses and encouragements. The voicing of desire. So I reward him. I shrug the wetsuit off one shoulder, then the other, so that my breasts are hanging free like pearls, the cool air making my nipples peak.

"You—" His throat works as he shifts in his seat, a long angle straining against his swim trunks. He's getting hard. "Are you sure?"

I nod and bend over to shuck the wetsuit off my legs.

But he shakes his head, his voice rough, pleading. "Ilsa—"

"Shh," I say, pressing a finger to his lips. "Just—don't talk."

And pushing him flat against the backrest of the fighting chair, I swing one knee over his lap, then the other, so I'm straddling him. The old sportfishing chair creaks in complaint.

Kaipo's eyes have grown enormous, the breath sawing in and out of him. He looks ready for that blackout now. He looks up at me, hands digging into the armrests to restrain himself, as I grind against him, rubbing myself along his shaft, nothing but the thin nylon of his trunks between us. His eyes flutter, but he does not look away. His nails claw into wood.

I like it. I'm filled with a wild urge to show my gratitude, to reward him.

"This is what you've wanted, isn't it?" I whisper, rushing the smoky words into his ear. "You've dreamed about this, haven't you?"

He jerks his head in a nod, taking his bottom lip between his teeth. "Mmhmm."

I drop my head lower, my silver hair falling over him, my lips almost against the shellwork of his ear. "You can touch me if you want, Kaipo Kalawai'a."

He lets out a low, agonized groan and lifts his hands from the armrests, places them on my hips with the reverence of a released prisoner. "Fuck," he whispers, the word a growl, and his fingers press into my flesh.

"That's right," I urge, my hand dipping inside his swim trunks as I continue grinding. Then he's hot and huge in my hand, and he sucks in a breath. I begin to stroke him. "That's right, big boy."

He curses again and lifts his head to kiss me, but I pull back. "Uh-uh." I waggle a finger. "Not yet."

His lips peel back, a ferocious grin around gritted teeth, and his brown eyes never leave my face as I take him out of his trunks. Then I'm sinking onto him, the exquisiteness of him inside me making me gasp. His jaw drops, that grin still teasing his lips as he watches me. The hunger there exhilarating. It breaks all restraint I have left. I begin riding him, both hands gripping the top of the backrest, the sensation of his fullness inside me driving me crazy. I rake my wet hair out of my face and lock eyes with him, pouring all my yearning and sultry want into that look. Everything I've been holding back and telling myself I was wrong to feel. Because here, now, in this moment, it doesn't. It doesn't feel wrong to feel this way. It doesn't feel wrong to share this with him. It doesn't feel wrong to celebrate this thing between us.

Not wrong.

He sees it. He returns it, mouth open in awe and desire, in breathless wonderment that this is truly happening. It sends a frisson of satisfaction through me, a slippery and depraved excitement. It is happening, isn't it? And the words echo in my head: *It's happening, this is happening.* A faint ring to it of ruin and despair. Of reckless jubilation in the face of destruction. But also tenderness. The knowledge that this may be all we get. That this is our moment. His hands rise to cradle my face, and I slow above him. The gentleness of it, the raw feeling—it's too much. My eyes sting. I shut them and drop my head, rubbing my forehead against his, leaving a streak of cold tears on his skin. *This is how it was*, I think. *This is how it felt to be alive.* When I move on him again, it's with renewed want, a deep basking in the pleasure of it. I fling my head back, a moan escaping my lips as Kaipo takes my breasts in his hands, his mouth sucking one nipple until it's hard and tingling in his mouth. I gasp. He slaps my ass, making the flesh bounce. And then I'm bouncing on him, harder and faster, my cheeks clapping on his lap. The way he watches me now with those smoldering eyes makes me want to both exult and hide my face with embarrassment.

The things this man does to me.

His fighting chair can't seem to take it. It creaks and creaks, comically loud, and Kaipo can't hold back a quip, because he's Kaipo: "I really need to oil this."

I let out a snort of laughter, almost falling off him in a fit of giggles, and have to clap a hand over his grinning mouth. "Shut *up*," I grit, pointing a finger in his face, my eyes huge with mock threat.

But I can't keep it together. His humor undoes me, as it always has, and there's no going back. My laugh turns into a moan as I bow over him, thighs clenching as the pleasure builds and builds, a tsunami that breaks past all boundaries and sets every cell in my body fizzing. Kaipo rests his brow against mine and grips my hips, keeping me there in that place of delicious torture, and that does it. The ecstasy spills over and my core tightens as I come, again and again, bucking on his lap until I'm spent, slumped against him, my legs quivering. And Kaipo bunches a hand in my hair and holds me there, wrapped in his arms.

After a while, when there's only the soft lap and splash of water against the hull, a sudden self-consciousness hits me, an instinct to hide, and I push myself away from him. I stand on coltish and trembling legs, but I don't get far at all. Because Kaipo's not having it.

"No, you don't," he says and sweeps a hand under my knees, scoops me up and sits back so I'm curled in a ball on his lap. "You're staying right here."

If I could flush, I would. I relax against him, my ear to his chest, and listen to the familiar refrain of his heart. *Boom-boom, boom-boom.* The opening and closing of its chambers, the meaty pumping of blood. Strong. Alive. *Him.* I have never been this close to it. The thunder of it fills me, rocking me like a lullaby.

It sounds like Kaipo. It sounds like home.

It sounds like where I belong.

I lay a hand against his chest and trace a small scar there with my fingertips, feeling the heat of his life seeping into my cold flesh. I am suffused with emotion.

My throat collapses around the word, turning it raw and scratchy: "Kaipo . . ."

But he shakes his head above me. "You don't have to say it."

"I know." I nod against his chest. "But I need to. I'll never be able to live with myself if I don't."

After a long period of silence, he lets out a breath, as if resigning himself to a sentence, an inevitable fate. "Okay."

I push myself up so I can look at him. My eyes dart back and forth between his, taking him in. He looks solemn, ready, as if in preparation for a ritual that will be both life-affirming and fatal.

The words are soft as they leave my lips: "I love you, Fishman."

His beard twitches, and he touches my cheek, his eyes bright and suddenly glassy. "I love you, Shipwright."

My heart surges in my chest. And, finally, I allow it to happen. I dip my head, my lips parted in hunger, in breathless want.

And then I'm kissing him.

I knew. I knew if I let this happen, there would be no going back. No returning from the certainty of it. The certainty of my love for him. And it's true. His soft, full lips meet mine with the same hunger, their warmth startling and delicious. They part wider, and then there's the clean click of his teeth against mine and the shy flick of his tongue, playful and desiring. I open my mouth to that ache and moan, the sound helpless, primal. I expect him to play with me, just like his jokes. I expect teasing, and pleasant torment. Instead, his kiss slips deeper, his hand burying in my hair as he holds me to him, a long, unbroken pressure of bittersweet tenderness. As if he were savoring every detail of this fleeting moment, committing it to memory. A treasure to cherish in the long days ahead.

When I break the kiss, tears trembling in my eyes and pluming on my lashes, I look down.

"I'm sorry," I croak, dashing a wrist across my face. "I just—I don't know how I'd respect myself if I—"

"Hey, I get it." He holds my face with both hands, brow lowered as he locks eyes to make sure every word sinks in. "I don't have any regrets."

My heart pinches. Guilt comes, in great overwhelming waves, and my face screws up. "Thank you," I manage, my lip trembling. "Thank you for everything. Thank you for saving me. Thank you for helping me let go. Meeting you was . . ."

But I can't finish. Small, hiccupping sobs catch in my throat, and he pulls my head down so he can press his lips to my brow in a blaze of warmth. "It's all right," he whispers against my skin. "It's all right."

But it's not. Not even close.

I thought I knew everything. All along, I thought I knew what I was fighting for. I thought Reinhard was my purpose. My soulmate. But now—now I am cast into doubt and uncertainty. Now I don't know what I was fighting for all these years.

Now, at the last moment, I may have found what I want.

And I have to let it go.

Kaipo holds me as I cry, his rough hand running through my hair, tucking it behind my ear and down the curve of my shaking shoulder in a spill of quicksilver. Slow, slow. Reassuring. Never stopping as my sobs run their course, as they turn into quiet sniffles and eventually long, heavy sighs. He knows what I need. He knows I need to let this out, and that nothing's required of him here other than to be the rock my grief can dash itself against. Because he's a straight up-and-down man.

And when it's gone, and the storm has passed, my body sags in his arms, sore and bone-tired yet feeling more cleansed than it has ever been. I feel as if I am melting into him; I have never felt this close to anyone. It's terrifying.

"You promise me something?" he asks at last.

My voice comes out a miserable croak. "What?"

I can feel his smile above me as he strokes my hair. "Whatever you choose to do next, please hire someone to run things and be a hands-off CEO. Because you're a real fucking terror of a micromanager."

I can't help it: I snort out a laugh, and the knot in my heart eases a little. "Noted." I shift so I can look up at him from his lap, my voice soft with an unsaid thanks. "I think I'd be different now, though."

He looks down at me, eyes twinkling. "I think so, too."

And we stare at each other like that for a long moment, an unseen thread tugging at our hearts.

Then a telltale smirk tugs at his lips, and I grin, knowing something's about to happen. *"What?"* I snort.

But he doesn't reply. In one breathless movement, he's stood from the chair with me swept against him, and a little squeal escapes me. I've never made any noise even remotely resembling a squeal before.

Then he's whirled about so he can set me in his place on the fighting chair. I blink. "What are you doing?"

He gives me a rakish smirk. "I'm going to find out."

My stomach drops. "Find out what?"

There's a sharp tug as he ties my wrist to the armrest with a hank of sailing line, yanking the knot tight. He winks. "If you're able to let go of control."

I gape. "What are you—"

But before I can say anything, he's gently but firmly placed my other wrist on an armrest and is tying it there with more line. Then, his eyes locked on mine, he tugs my legs wide—my stomach flutters—and placing my heels on the wooden paddle of the footrest, he ties my ankles so I'm spread-eagled and vulnerable.

Oh.

Heat creeps up my neck. The realization following it, turning my mind filthy.

I know what he's about to do. It makes everything inside me squirm in terror and delight.

I sit there on his fighting chair, helpless and trembling, as he crouches before me. His grin is a wicked thing. "Now," he says, and slides his hands under my ass and lowers his head so he's breathing on me down there, making my body turn into goosepimples. "I'm going to take every last ounce of control away from you."

And he does.

# TWENTY-SEVEN

At sunset the following day, we reach Transmarinia.

It's small, a hump of black against the pink clouds of day's end. But seeing it rivets me to the spot, and I feel my heart surge in my chest, my hand grip a support strut as I stare from the *Kanaloa*'s tuna tower bridge.

Kaipo at the helm beside me watches my face.

Something is happening to my body. Sparks and chills, followed by a spreading numbness as that black hulk grows larger and larger.

The site of so much pain.

The site of my doom.

The world has deepened into a gray, bleak dusk by the time we glide along the coastline of Transmarinia. A jolt stiffens my spine as the shipyard comes into view. The cranes and slipways, the dry docks and warehouses holding half-constructed yachts, all left dark and abandoned. It's been shuttered in my absence, left to gather rust like a ship graveyard. The end of an era.

Kaipo squints against the wind, his mane of gold-glinting hair blown back from his brow. "So that's where they kept you."

I nod, not trusting myself to speak.

We're here. At long last, we're back. To the place I swore I'd never return to.

Welcome home, Shipwright.

Kaipo glances at me, an inscrutable expression behind his eyes, and steers the *Kanaloa* upcoast.

Next, the beach with its colorful strandkorbs, those wicker beach chairs upholstered in striped canvas. They line the shore, empty and strewn with sand, their sunblind hoods fluttering forlornly in the sea breeze like a haunted resort. I think of my conversation with Arie there, that conversation that took me away from this place and back again, and my jaw tightens.

Transmarinia is not large, perhaps a few miles long, but it's getting darker by the second. So night is falling by the time we approach the island's northernmost point. The island is higher here, rising up in cliffs of black rock shining wetly in the moonlight. I haven't been up this way, never wandered beyond the eastern shore where I'd been remanded all those years, too locked inside my rage and depression to bother. It's wilder up here, the tops of the cliffs covered in a forest of pine and maple, overgrown and haggard and windswept, their branches whistling and whacking in the night. All this lost though in the dull boom of the surf against the rocky shore.

And there, far up a cliff jutting out into the sea, a color that doesn't belong.

It's orange. High in a black cliff face. At night. Orange.

It flickers and dances, pulsing like a coal. Like flame.

A cave, I realize. A crevice in the rock, like an entrance to an old pirate hideout.

And I think: *Reinhard*.

Prickles of electricity run all up and down my body.

"Transmarinia," I whisper. "North Point."

Kaipo follows my gaze and swallows.

We put into a small cove around a bend and follow the rocky shoreline in sleek black wetsuits, bare feet gripping rock. A storm must have hit the island recently; the shore is strewn with shells and driftwood and small anonymous bones, huge boulders covered in ropes of seaweed and giant black eggs nestled in kelp. A briny, riotous, pungent reek.

We kneel behind a boulder, the freezing surf surging about our feet, and fitting a pair of binoculars to my eyes I glass the cliff.

After a moment, I find it again: the flare of firelight on rock. And the cleft there, with a landing of sorts, a ledge wide enough for two men to stand abreast.

I lower the glasses, frowning. "I don't like it. It's too quiet."

Kaipo eyes the shoreline, the clifftops, a grim expression on his face. "Nothing for it though, is there?"

"No," I grumble, tucking the binoculars away. "There isn't."

I slip the strap of the atlas tube over my shoulder, and we've no more stood from our crouch than there's a clicking on rock and something wet and cold brushes my foot.

I glance down, but whatever it was is already gone, skittering amongst the boulders.

Then there's a squeak and a rat, black and bald-tailed, plops onto a boulder to my left and darts off. It seemed to have dropped from the sky. Seconds later, another falls to my right.

And now that I'm listening, there's another sound on the night air, something I at first took for the sullen crash of the waves. A low chorus of squeaks, high-pitched screeches.

All the hairs on the back of my neck stand on end, and I lift my eyes to look.

All along the tumbled rocky shoreline between us and the cliff, eyes watch us. Dozens of them. Rats perch on the seaweed-draped rocks with whiskered noses scenting the air. Rats splash in the tidepools. They boil out of holes in the cliff in an endless deluge, squeaking and biting and crawling over each other. And when I lift my eyes higher and higher, I find that the whole shoreline of boulders heaped against the cliffs is covered in a thick carpet of rats. A colony of them. Hundreds of them. Thousands. A seething mass of vermin flung in a squirming pile out here to hold communion with the moon, or with me. A vile, unreal vision. A nightmare.

At night, this is their beach, not ours.

My stomach bottoms out. A sickly warm nausea rises in my throat, making me gag. My ankles suddenly itch like mad.

A warm hand slides into mine: Kaipo is staring at me closely, putting two and two together. "It's okay," he says, and tugs my hand. "Come on. I got you."

But I shake my head, give his hand a squeeze and gently slip out of his grasp.

"Thanks," I say, and smile at him. "But I need to do this for myself."

He blinks and nods, understanding, and steps away.

Side by side, we make our way across the beach to the cliff.

At first, it's not hard to avoid the rats. Even in the last light of day, we can make out their black shapes, the pale whip of their tails as they scurry into crevices. But then they grow thicker and thicker, inescapable clots clinging to the boulders above the crashing surf. Soon, I have to nudge them aside with my foot, gingerly angle my toes down to find purchase on the next boulder. I am high-stepping amongst a seething, squeaking plain of twitching noses and scrabbling claws. Something cold slithers across my foot and I clench my hands. Small, hairy bodies surge about my calves and I bite down a whimper. That itching sensation is making my skin crawl now. A few rats tumble into the water, screeching, and I shut my eyes and hear Reinhard screaming my name.

A few feet to my left, Kaipo watches me, his face aching with sympathy. But I cannot rely on him now.

I need to face this.

They won't bite me, I remind myself. There's no reason to. They won't climb my suit. They won't pour down my throat. They won't they won't they won't—

Small teeth nip my calf, and something inside me breaks.

I lurch forward, stiff-backed and thinking of small hairy bodies covering me, swirling up Reinhard as blood gushes down his neck, and a scream is building against my pressed-together lips. I have to let it out, I have to, have to, have to—

Cold rock against my hands. The cliff. I slump against it and hitch in a sob of a breath, eyes squinched shut, fingernails clawing stone and tendrils of roots.

After a long, long time, my breathing slows, and a big hand rests on my back, rubs small, soothing circles there.

Kaipo. Watching me with the kindest, proudest eyes I've ever seen.

He smiles. "Ready?"

I nod.

Now the climb. We find handholds, small outcroppings to grip. We pull ourselves up, pressing our bodies flat like crabs, and let the rocks take our weight. They hold.

Higher now. Higher. Feeling many eyes on our skin. The din of the rats and sea below us. And another sound now: the crying of gulls.

As I climb, I glimpse glittering eyes, rats wedged into crevices in the cliff.

Something falls on me, gets tangled in my hair, little feet scratching my face as it squeaks in my ear. For a moment I think it will fall, but it's too stuck. It jerks and scrabbles and scratches, a wild animal rankness crawling up my nostrils, sliding over my sinuses, coating my tongue. A hairless tail whips at my cheek, grazes my ear canal in hideous intimacy. Small teeth nick my neck and I remember fiendish fangs sinking into my flesh.

Kaipo crabs sideways to me across the cliff face, white with concern—

But I've already yanked the rat out of my hair, bashed it against rock and let it drop bonelessly below.

Kaipo stares, his breath on my face. "You okay?"

I nod, remembering fangs, that shadowy plague-bringer, and think, *Fuck you.*

"We can take a moment—" Kaipo begins.

"Let's go."

It's not long before we see the orange light flickering above us. I reach the ledge first. I get my elbows over the lip, pull myself up. Then I'm pulling Kaipo up after me, the two of us staggering there a moment in the whipping wind.

We share a smile.

When I turn around to face the crevice, the man is suddenly stepping out of its shadow into the moonlight, as surprised by my appearance as I am by his. A guard. One of Reinhard's captors. His cigarette newly lit, a rifle slung on his back. His fangs glinting in the moonlight. He goes for the rifle, but I'm faster. I grab it and use it as leverage to flip the guard onto his back. He's about to rise when Kaipo sinks down to one knee beside me and plunges a tactical knife up to the hilt into the vampire's heart. I clamp my hand over his mouth to stifle his scream.

Waves boom against the cliff. Gulls caw. Kaipo and I crouch there, listening.

No sounds of movement. No one's been alerted.

Kaipo drags the body to the ledge and flings it off the cliff onto the rocks below. It disappears without a sound. Kaipo doesn't linger to watch. He returns to take the rifle from me, unbolts the barrel to check it's loaded, rebolts it and nods.

It's time.

I look down the rock cleft flickering with warm orange light. This is it. It's all come to this. All of it. Everything.

This is where I find all the answers. This is where I leave everything behind.

Everyone behind.

I look over at Kaipo. He's watching me, his shoulders set, his eyes wounded and knowing, his wild mane of hair blowing in the wind off the sea. Loyal to the last.

"You don't have to come, you know," I tell him. "You don't have to . . . see this."

"There might be more of them in there," he says simply, and tucks the butt of the rifle into his shoulder, winks with gallant humor. "Don't want to miss out on all the fun."

My heart pinches. I want to kiss him so badly in this moment. I want to wipe away that hurt and tell him no,

I've changed my mind, let's go back, let's not see what's waiting for us in there.

I know I'll lose myself forever if I do.

And turning my back on Kaipo Kalawai'a, I lead him into the cave.

# TWENTY-EIGHT

The opening to the cave is low, its craggy ceiling only inches above our heads, a tunnel into fitful gloom. I follow it to the find the source of the light.

It's not a fire, like I thought, but candles. Dozens, fifty of them. Set into recesses in the rock or in branches of old candelabra, dripping stalactites of melted wax. But even before the light, it's the smell that hits me, rank and overpowering, strong enough to make me want to cover my nose. The smell of rotting meat. That's when I see the bones. They're scattered in small piles everywhere, some still stained red and clotted with gristle. Heaped in corners, beside an old pallet on the floor. On the far side of the cave where a naked figure crouches with its back to us, hunched over something in its hands.

There's a greedy slurping sound, and the figure's sunken ribs wheeze in and out with the force of its guzzling, shoulders buckling like something caught in the act of love.

Cold prickles of dread shoot down my spine.

Kaipo steps up beside me, rifle aimed, and the figure whips its head around to glare at us through a tangle of unwashed hair.

The face is smeared in gore. The sideburns matted. The talonlike nails clutching the dead rat cracked and yellow.

But it's Reinhard, all the same.

My chest tightens. The world contracts. There's no air in the world left for my lungs.

"Reinhard?" I whisper.

I take a step forward. Another. As if approaching a wild animal. Reinhard drops the rat and swallows. Those blue eyes the same, the only thing that have remained unchanged over the long years. Like the heart of a fire.

My own blur up. "*Reinhard?* Darling?"

Kaipo lowers the rifle and looks away, the muscles at the corners of his jaw pulsing.

I dart a glance at him. I don't know why, but self-consciousness—something much like embarrassment—burns in my throat.

Or maybe those are just tears.

"Reinhard . . ." The word escapes in a sob, and I rush forward to embrace him.

But he scrambles back to huddle in a corner, hunches his head down into his scrawny shoulders, hands rubbing his arms. "N-n-no!" he blurts in a helpless stutter, and shakes his head. "D-d-don't. I'm n-n-not—not w-w-worthy."

I blink, frozen in place. My heart collapses in my chest. The beginnings of humiliation creep up my neck.

"What?" I shake my head, kneel down to touch him. "Darling, that's non—"

"No!" He jerks away from my touch. His hands clutching his face now, long nails clawing in shame. My Reinhard. My upright, well-spoken man-about-town. Stuttering in terror. "I m-must stay here. Master w-wants me to stay here."

"Master?" I wet my lips, run a tongue over my fangs. "Volok's gone, Reinhard. He's dead."

But Reinhard shakes his head. "Must honor M-M-Master's wishes. Must suh-suh-stay *here* . . ."

I blink. Something in my chest crumples. "But . . . it's me. Don't you . . . don't you remember me?" I can't help it: tears sheen my eyes. Tears that have gone unshed for centuries. "Aren't *I* worth it?"

He twitches to look at me now, and hope surges in me. He's in there. He has to be. Surely, he remembers—

But he turns away and rocks in place, crooning to himself. "M-M-Master would be angry. C-c-can't have M-Master angry . . ."

I sit back on my heels, a numbness working its way through me, up my chest, into my throat, fuzzing up my head. I have no thoughts anymore. That cottony fluff is a barrier between myself and the world, the need to recognize what is happening. Because it didn't happen. It can't have.

I can't have fought for centuries for this. I can't have sacrificed so much to be met with unrecognition, or denial, or whatever harrowing brand of terror and cowardice this is.

I'm not here. This isn't happening.

That isn't a touch on my shoulder.

"Hey." Kaipo crouches down beside me, the rifle stood at his side. His face wavers between disgust and sorrowful compassion as he looks between me and what has become of my husband. "Come on." He tugs at my elbow. "This is no longer your Reinhard. Whatever he was—whatever man you loved—Volok broke him. You need to let him go."

I don't know if I can ever move again. But, it turns out, I can. I stand, and Kaipo steers me about, walks me on senseless, shuffling feet back toward the mouth of the cave. Away from the candlelight and the bones and what huddles against the far cave wall. Away from the first man who ever loved me.

Away from the man whose life gave me purpose.

I stop in place. "I can't." My lower lip trembles, and I fly my eyes up into Kaipo's face. "I can't leave him."

It takes a moment for it to penetrate Kaipo. The staggering hurt. He looks as if the wind has been knocked out of him. He runs a hand down his face and glances at Reinhard. At me. "You sure?"

How astonishing—how breathtaking—the power two words can have on you.

I want to hold his face in my hands. I want to bury myself in his arms and beg for forgiveness. I want to tell him that I have never been happier than I have been with him.

Instead, I whisper, "I'm so sorry."

He winces and looks down, nods as he drags a foot back, drops it in place. "You, uh . . ." He props his hands on his hips, dashes a wrist under his nose and sniffs. "You don't owe him anything, you know."

My lips downturn, a fat swell of pity stretching my ribcage, and I lay a hand on his cheek. "I owe him everything."

Kaipo shuts his eyes, holds my hand there. After a moment, he cracks his lids to look at me. "And what about me?"

The tears come now, scalding fire. I place a hand on his chest, feel that heart beating with more pain than I have ever felt in another. It unravels my voice. "I owe you everything, too."

Kaipo's face is twitching all over now, close to catastrophic collapse. He nods in acknowledgment of my words, unable to meet my eyes. He shifts his weight back and forth in place, draws in a breath that's halfway between a sob and a laugh at this astounding pain, and for a moment I see in him the lost young man who was abandoned by his family.

I fling my arms around his neck, my fingers curled in his hair, and let him hold me one last time.

The universe stops.

Then he can't take it anymore. He gently disengages, cups the back of my head and presses his lips to my brow, just like he did the last time he said goodbye.

*(I love you, Shipwright.)*

*(I love you, Fishman.)*

I shut my eyes. But tears are leaking out from under my lids, all the same. One streaks fast down my cheek.

How can you live through a moment like this? How can a heart endure it?

Then Kaipo is moving past me, striding stiff-backed into the shadows of the cave mouth. Far away, the sea crashes. A gull cries. And then there's no more sound. No more footsteps.

He's gone.

# TWENTY-NINE

I'm not sure how long I stand there. After a while, I become aware that I have my back to my husband, my hands over my eyes, my shoulders hitching in barely suppressed sobs. The sorrow crests inside my chest like a wave and demolishes me, wrenching everything loose. My dignity. My sanity. My defenses against despair.

Kaipo.

I pushed him away. Again. I'll never get him back. I may have destroyed him with that kind of abandonment.

I may have just made the biggest mistake of my life.

But I made my choice. Leaving my husband would have destroyed me, too. I would never have been able to love Kaipo through that guilt, which would only have been another kind of abandonment, this one far worse as it would be stretched out over years, an excruciatingly slow drifting away that would leave Kaipo a shell of who he was.

Best to cut if off clean now. This is the way it must be.

When the hiccupping breaths subside, I tilt my head back and look up at the ceiling, will the tears back into my eyes.

Then, brushing the salty tracks from my face, I turn about and attend to my husband.

He's still huddled against the rock wall, still rocking slightly. But he watches me now, wary and with a glimmer of awareness. I sit cross-legged in front of him, unhook the atlas tube from my back and set it aside. Then I take one of his hands in mine, begin to rub the dirty lines of his palm with my thumb.

"I missed you," I say.

When I look up at him, his rocking has stopped, his brows drawn together.

That's something.

"I felt so much guilt. I gave myself a hard time for not being able to save you. And I see now that you might have felt the same way." I risk another look at him, my voice faint with hope. All this time, I had held onto the fanatic's belief that he would be exactly as I remembered him. That is what I needed to get me through everything. But in my weaker moments, I had been more realistic. There had been the worry, of course, of what would happen when we reunited. Of the possibility of being confronted with someone who had become a stranger over the many intervening years, maybe even someone I could no longer love. That, in short, there would be disappointment. And then there would be the awkward and almost humiliating process of getting to know each other again. The tentative overtures, the fear that it would never be the same. But this turn of events—as horrible as it may be—is almost freeing. This simplifies things, lays out a clear path forward. I can set about undertaking the rather uncomplicated task of caring for him, nursing him back to who he was. No matter that this obscuring trauma prolongs the question of whether or not this is still the Reinhard I fell in love with.

No. This is how I make amends. This is how I atone for any feelings of failure.

Perhaps, I even believe that if he doesn't recover, that will be a fate I deserve.

As long as certain fantasies are preserved.

"Did you fight for me?" I ask, not quite looking at him. "Did you try to get back to me?"

After a long moment, he nods.

I drop my eyes, my body humming with relief, contentment. I almost smile.

"But they stopped you," I prompt, though I don't check for his nod again.

The awareness, yes, of nudging this narrative in the direction I want. A narrative which suits my needs in this moment.

Which allows me to live with this.

Perhaps I'm the broken one, after all.

I rub his hand. "What did they do to you?"

But his hand stiffens at that, slowly closes in on itself.

I hold on. "Hey, it's okay. We're free now. We can put all that behind us. We can start over." I lean in, catching his gaze. "Okay?"

He watches me, those acetylene-flame eyes darting back and forth between mine. The closest I'll get to a yes.

I smile. "Okay." I lift his hand, press my lips to it. "Let's find you some clothes."

There's not much in the cave. No furniture except for the candelabra and the straw pallet that appears to be his bed. Nothing amongst the ricks of sticky bones. But the cave is bigger than I thought: another chamber breaks off from it into darkness. From that darkness, a faint glow emanates, like some undersea phenomena.

I follow the light.

It comes from a grid of monitors hooked up against a wall. Some dark, others buzzing with static. The rest are tuned to camera feeds. They show all angles of Transmarinia. The beach with its strandkorbs. The shipyard with its warehouses and shops. Even the inside of my old office.

Which would mean—

"What is this?" I've gone rigid. The backs of my arms prickle with chill. My voice hardens into a demand. "Reinhard. What is this?"

The voice that comes from behind me is very different. Calm, measured, almost mournful. "It w-w-was the only way. That was the c-c-covenant I had to m-make. I watch you, and you l-l-l-live."

I turn to face him. He's standing now, a shadow outlined by flickering candlelight. A stranger.

"You're the spy Volok had on Transmarinia," I breathe.

He says nothing.

My stomach turns over. A sickly sweat pops out on my brow. The words come out from between teeth chattering with adrenaline. "But that would mean you—you were the one who betrayed me. You're the reason Volok knew I was coming and—"

Buried me in fire and water. Kept me forever drowning beneath the sea.

Which also means—

"You're the reason I lost my chance to see Volok slain." I huff out a breath of horror and stunned admiration, too dizzy to even grasp yet at the totality of this treachery. "You took away my closure. You took away my *peace*."

He takes a step toward me. There's a slight wheedling tone in his voice now, a plea for understanding. "It h-had to be this way. You don't know h-h-h-him like I do. You don't know wh-wh-what he's like."

I look at him. The man who was my husband but who is no longer my husband. Because a husband could not do what he has done. "But he's gone," I say. (My husband's gone.) "Volok's gone."

Reinhard shakes his head. "Not his buh-buh-blood father. N-n-n-not the Grandmaker."

The name brings a chill to my skin. Even a wind skirls into the cave at its invocation, heeling the candleflames over in a wavering of shadows.

Reinhard takes another step closer. "Did you r-r-really think Volok was the oldest of us? How w-would there still be any of our k-k-kind, if Volok was the first?"

And he lifts something he's been holding behind his back. The atlas.

The candleflames blur and sharpen again. My heart knocks in my ribs.

He skims his talons along the tube's length. "He's been suh-suh-sleeping for m-many years. But it's time for him to f-f-finally wake." He uncaps the tube, slides the rolled-up atlas out a few inches, turns it so the gilt lettering of the title catches in the candlelight. Satisfied, he slides it back in. "And now we know h-h-how to f-find him."

The candles gutter again. Ice shoots tendrils down my spine.

This was their plan all along. This is how they supplant Arie. By bringing back the oldest and most powerful of us. All they needed was a map to find his location.

And I brought it right to them, like the fool I am.

What idiocy.

Reinhard lifts his brow to stare at me with those haunted blues. "You've m-m-met him already. We b-both have. He's our f-father too, after all."

Our father.

Suddenly, my skin itches, and I see a shadow gliding toward me on a tide of rats. That shadow that glided out from behind Volok and his translator, in our shipwright's shop all those years ago.

The shadow that took my life away from me.

I sway in place, my nose tingling. Bile rises in my throat. I feel tiny nails and teeth all over my body.

"No," I say, almost a snivel, and shake my head in useless denial. "That can't be . . ."

Reinhard watches me with both pity and hope in his face.

"There's no suh-suh-standing against them, Ilsa. I t-t-tried. But you d-d-don't know wh-what they're l-l-like." He swallows and offers the atlas, his old wedding band winking on his ring finger. "Be with me. We can be us again. They'll f-forgive you if you buh-bring this to them. They're coming n-n-now."

He juts his chin over my shoulder, and I look.

On one of those monitors, a fuzzy image of the moonlit sea outside. It's hard to make out at first. The image blinks out in a fit of static and bounces back. And then I see it. Something on that sea bathed in moonlight, getting closer. A ship I know all too well. Black as a hearse. Carbon-fibre masts raking the stars.

The *Keep*.

Volok's old ship. The flagship of the Sons of Volok.

The ship that blew up my life.

All the skin on my body breaks out in gooseflesh.

When I turn back to Reinhard again, his lips seam in a tentative smile, and for the first time I see his fangs. "We c-c-can be husband and w-wife again."

Husband and wife.

I have the absurd urge to laugh. What does he mean? He's made a mockery of our marriage. Of my life.

I could lose myself in that, I know. I could let myself be consumed by that anger. It would be enough to power a thousand lifetimes.

All I have to do is give into it.

And now, I give into something else: a tumult of intrusive thoughts, all those old nightmares roaring back, Reinhard and Kaipo slamming together in my brain into an incoherence of pasts and possible futures, paths to take or not take.

# THIRTY

Holding Reinhard's hand as we walk the snowy streets of Wismar. Men tip their hats to us as they pass. Reinhard is respected, our courtship is acknowledged, and I am cocooned in a feeling of sweet contentment. I will build a life with this man. I will drag myself out of poverty and the evil star I have struggled under. I have made it. This is the life I have always wanted. I have found love.

# THIRTY-ONE

Kaipo sitting close to me on the tuna tower, knees brushing, baring his soul. Teaching me about the love and hate within families, putting words to my rumination. Each pained sentence a starburst of revelation, a sacrifice for clarity between us. No man has ever fought for my understanding. No man has fought for my heart.

# THIRTY-TWO

Fangs sinking into flesh, Reinhard screaming, the rats overflowing, Volok tittering like a flirt. My rage is born.

# THIRTY-THREE

Kaipo sitting in his fighting chair, fishing rod in hand, reeling in a catch. The sun sparkles on the sea, Kaipo turns to me, and his smile is brighter than the water. Some catches are caught without them knowing.

# THIRTY-FOUR

Taking Reinhard's hand in marriage again. Letting that man—what that man has turned into—take me to the altar once more. I find safety in that union. Even use that union, perhaps, for vengeance still.

# THIRTY-FIVE

Kaipo going down on one knee on the *Kanaloa* and proposing to me.

# THIRTY-SIX

Using the atlas for my own purposes. I sneak away from my bridal bed with Reinhard to the coffinside of that ur-fiend, the original source of all my pain. I slide back the lid in a grating of stone to reveal that dread figure reposing in a squirming of maggots, and lift my stake. One plunge to end everything. To put an end to my anger. Forever.

# THIRTY-SEVEN

Kaipo taking me to his diving cliffs on Hawaii to marry me.

# THIRTY-EIGHT

The stake plunging. And my anger ending. Forever.

# THIRTY-NINE

Teasing Kaipo about the gray hairs sneaking into his beard, placing my hand to his aging cheek as our children run around us on a beach in Cozumel.

# FORTY

Or my anger does not end.

# FORTY-ONE

Curled up in bed with Kaipo, hands held, listening to his lovely heart slow into silence as all that high-humored life leaves his wrinkled and white-bearded face.

# FORTY-TWO

Which life do I choose?

# FORTY-THREE

"Ilsa?"

I blink. I feel as if I'm exploding with heartache, with all these lives lived or unlived, a backlog of memories and what-ifs. And Reinhard is there, really there, waiting for my answer. For me to choose an ending to all these tales.

Maybe that's what these ruminations have been for all along. Not something to be wholly resisted and rejected. But embraced, acknowledged and accepted, used to honor what's come before and reason out the path ahead.

Reinhard lifts the atlas, and I step forward and grip the plastic tube.

He lets out a shallow breath, and with it centuries of shame and trepidation. His eyes crinkle in a smile. Our fingers, on the tube, graze each other.

The world stills in a lush, trembling moment.

And ripping the tube from Reinhard Knackenkusser, I dash toward the cave mouth and the cliff beyond.

"Ilsa!"

Too late. I'm already leaping off the cliff into the night, and I'm praying I make it past the boulders as I fall, and fall, and fall through the salt-blown air, like the reckless fool I am.

All I've ever done is fall.

# FORTY-FOUR

Down from my mother's womb, slipping out of my father's hands, onto the floor in a slime of blood, wailing.

# FORTY-FIVE

Down into the frosty manure of Wismar's gutters, the other street urchins laughing.

# FORTY-SIX

Down into the sawdust in our shipwright's shop, blood and rat fur in my mouth.

# FORTY-SEVEN

Down, down, down like a flaming star into Sardinia's deep to slumber.

# FORTY-EIGHT

Down into haunted fathoms as penance for constructing a castle of horrors.

# FORTY-NINE

Down into the mists of a sinkhole to confront my blackest fears.

# FIFTY

Down and away from my husband into the roaring surf of the Baltic Sea.

# FIFTY-ONE

And I rise.

# FIFTY-TWO

The cold crush of water. Deep black. A chaos of bubbles and white froth. The tide like a fist trying to smack me against the boulders.

And then, like a baptism, air again.

I burst up into cool wind on my cheeks, cast a glance back at the craggy shoreline. The rats still there, squeaking, tails swishing, peepers glowing at me in the moonlight.

And high up, against a lick of orange, the silhouette of Reinhard watching me.

A dream. A nightmare. Another life.

But I don't care about that. Because a landslide is occurring within me, an avalanche of everyday wonders rushing back, loosed from behind the relentless hum of rumination that had kept me from being present all these years.

The beauty of lunar halos. A fresh snow. Sandfall in blue holes. The curlings of wood from an easel. A good weld. The pleasant gutturality of German. Sheet lightning. Feet in warm sand. Sperm whales. The milky smell of babies. A first kiss. The slopes of a lover's shoulders. The hope of trees. Sunrise.

All of it. All at once and overwhelming, a sweet rush of life narrowing my throat.

And there's only one person I want to share it with.

I whip about, shouldering the strap of the atlas' drafting tube as I look up and down the coastline of Transmarinia.

But it's not there. The *Kanaloa* is not there.

Kaipo did it. He left. He's really gone.

Dull shock sets in. My eyes burn. A small, selfish part of me had really believed he would stay. But what did I expect? Of course he'd leave after how I treated him. Why wouldn't he?

Choking down a lump in my throat, I look out to sea.

The *Keep* is still far off, a sinister shadow riding the moon reflected on the waves. But there are things setting out from it. Some form of outrunners. Headed straight toward me.

I tread water, listening. Far off, the high whine of engines, shining fiberglass hulls slapping across the waves.

Jet Skis.

And men straddle them, leaning over the handlebars into the wind. Pale of skin. Their mouths sharp.

In less than a minute, they'll be scooping me out of the water. In less than a minute, they'll be taking me back to the *Keep*. Where I'll be enslaved again. Maybe tortured, maybe killed.

No terror grips me this time, though. No despair. Only regret and self-reproach.

*I should have listened to you, Kaipo. I should have chosen you.*

I think of that life we could have had together. Sailing the oceans of the world in the *Kanaloa*. Snuggling up at night in the fighting chair and watching the stars. Diving in mystical kelp forests and deep-sea wrecks, sharing in marine wonders. Watching his face gather more laugh lines as he grew old, rubbing those grays in his beard with my thumb. Maybe it would have come true, us having a family. Maybe if this Grandmaker were slain, and I was turned back into a mortal woman, we would have had children together, watched them grow up on the beaches of Cozumel, and thinking of Kaipo as a father makes my stomach contort in a special kind of happy torment.

Maybe he would have asked me to turn him, and we would have spent forever together.

Or maybe I would have watched him die, as I foresaw, curled up in bed with him with our foreheads touching.

And I would have been grateful for every second of it.

The foremost Jet Ski is close now. I can make out the face of its rider, fangs bared in malicious anticipation, black hair blown back from his brow. He slows and leans, one hand swept out in a spreading of welcoming claws, ready to catch me.

I don't feel alarm. I am awash in strange serenity.

Because I am. I am grateful. For everything I did get with him.

What a gift. What luck.

I shut my eyes.

*(I love you, Fishman.)*

And a crack rings out across the sea.

I snap my eyes open to see the Jet Ski fly past me, its rider flopped back on the seat, eyes wide, a bloody crater drilled into his forehead.

I twist about.

A boat is surging around a bend in the coastline, making a beeline for me. It has a familiar sloped superstructure. A tuna tower. And at the tuna tower controls, a man with a wind-blown lion's mane stands with a sniper rifle ported at hip. He ejects a long shell casing and slides another one into the barrel, bolts it in.

My heart leaps with wild joy.

He didn't leave. He was never going to leave.

He stayed for me.

He waves a hand—"Climb on!"—and lowers his sniper rifle to squint through the sight again.

Urgency returns, slamming into me like a hurricane. I cut through the water as more gunshots ring out. Here and there, I glimpse bobbing Jet Skis, engines idling and riderless. But Kaipo can't hold them off for long.

They circle the *Kanaloa* like orcas, moving in an orchestration of death. One hops aboard. Another. "Kaipo!" I shout and surge forward.

I almost leap out of the water onto the swim deck. I take in the situation at a glance. Two Sons of Volok already up on the tuna tower. Kaipo is barely fending them off. One pins him to the helm, the sniper rifle between them, while the other scurries up the ladder.

The thought of losing Kaipo now brings on a terrifying clarity.

No hesitation: I snatch a harpoon from its rack, heave back and let fly.

The force is like a spear shot from a cannon. The Son of Volok pinning Kaipo is blasted off the tuna tower into the sea. For a moment, I catch Kaipo's register of surprise—before the other cultist is on him.

I'm right behind.

A blur of ladder rungs, and then I'm in that crow's nest with them. Kaipo's sniper rifle has been batted away, and he's braced his forearm against the cultist's throat to keep gleaming fangs from his neck.

They clack at him: *KAK KAK KAK*.

Protective anger blooms in me like a hydrogen bomb.

The cultist doesn't even see me coming. One moment, his fangs are nutcrackering toward Kaipo's jugular. The next, I've grabbed him and flung him bodily off the tuna tower—and onto a rack of harpoons below, the many spearheads erupting from his chest in a geyser of gore.

Kaipo gapes. He looks from the impaled corpse to me, breathing hard.

Then I'm crushing him to me in a tight hug, my lips pressed against his.

For a moment, he's too stunned to respond. Then his arms wrap around me, those big hands pressing me to him, fingers separated, with such firm and changing pressures that it leaves me in a state of giddy elation. Everything has changed. Everything has transformed. Happiness has poured back into the world. All things have been put right again.

I don't have to spend my life alone and in a constant state of heartbreak. Whatever comes now, I can face it. Because I'm with him. Kaipo. Forever.

I pull away, glowing with a breathless smile, and yet somehow shy. "You didn't leave," I whisper.

His deep brown eyes crinkle. "And you came back."

I clutch him. "I'm so sorry," I whisper. "I'm so sorry I hurt you. Thank you for never giving up on me."

But he draws a knuckle down my cheek, smiling that infectious smile I so love. "The best fish take the longest to catch."

I want to laugh, but my stomach is too busy flipping over. I drop my eyes, suddenly rueful. "You're right. I don't owe him anything. He's not the man he was."

He watches me, a knowing look of sadness in his eyes, but also pride. Waiting for me to finish.

So I do.

"I couldn't admit to myself what I felt. About you. About us. But I know now." I take a deep, even breath and plunge on. "I was afraid to be happy again. I was afraid I didn't deserve it. That I needed to punish myself. But I don't have to. Because what happened wasn't my fault. It never was. Love isn't something you should have to chase, or prove you're worthy of. It's just there. The way you've been."

Kaipo's eyes glisten. His nostrils flare, as if holding back a prickling of tears. He tucks a wet lock of hair behind my ear. "Are you showing your feelings, Ilsa Knackenkusser? Isn't that something Germans don't do?"

I snort and curl my fingers into his shirt. "Maybe you've changed me." I lift my head to look at him, serious again. "I'm so proud to know you, Kaipo. I feel so lucky to be loved by someone like you. And I promise: You'll never lose me. Ever. You will never be abandoned again. I'm immortal, anyway, so I'm afraid you're stuck with me for a while."

He throws back his head and lets out a choked laugh, making my heart soar. His eyes are far from dry when they meet mine again. "I guess Germans do humor after all."

I grin. "This one does, anyway. I wonder how that happened?"

His hand goes back to playing with my hair. "I wonder." He's beaming ear to ear now, and seeing him like that fills up every nook and cranny in me with pulsating warmth. I feel almost alive again. I am alive.

He's resurrected me.

He shakes his head. "I didn't know what I would have done if you didn't come back. I'm lost without you, Ilsa. I thought I'd never find family again. I never thought I'd feel belonging again. But with you . . ." His lip trembles, and my eyes sting. I tighten my fingers in his shirt, urging him on.

He draws in a long, wavery breath, lets it out. "You're my family, Ilsa. I felt it the moment I met you. And I will always choose you. Always."

My throat lumps up, and he cups the back of my head and draws my brow to his. I am heavy with love; I am light as air. Nothing in this world makes sense anymore.

But this does. This here makes sense. It always did.

Kaipo draws back, his smile promising a lifetime of laughter and diving and delicious mischief. Then he glances away from this extraordinary thing between us. Out at the sea, and what's approaching us. His lips thin into a line of displeasure. "We should go."

And with a frisson of shock, I remember.

The *Keep*. The Sons of Volok.

*The atlas*.

I unsling the drafting tube from my back with shaking fingers. "They've been after this all along. That's why they've been following us. It'll show them how to find the grandmaker of all nosferatu."

Kaipo's face stills as he studies the tube. "The Grandmaker?"

I nod, my voice growing soft. "He—he's my maker, too." I can't meet Kaipo's eyes, as if I've revealed an embarrassing secret, some indecent past act. So I clear my throat and go on. "They want to wake him and bring him back to power. That's how they plan to end Arie's reign."

Kaipo's gaze is steady, his voice wary. "And what's *your* plan?"

I look up at him, my bones thrumming with understanding. He's afraid. He's afraid that this Grandmaker will be my new Volok. That my rage has been revived and has found a new focus.

That this isn't over yet.

And he's right. It's not. But not in the way he thinks.

My heart swells; I'm unable to restrain a smile of radiant joy. How could I, when I finally understand? That this is the lesson I needed, all this time. That Kaipo is the lesson I needed.

That there will always be something to be angry about, and you will never let it go until you choose to.

"Nah," I say, and wrap my arms around his neck, pulling him close so our noses are touching. "I'm happy right here."

The impact this has on Kaipo is visceral and immediate. He draws in a big, shaky breath and lets out a little laugh of amazement. I can feel all his muscles trembling against me, as if he's finally let it go. That fear of unworthiness. That feeling of abandonment. That last, stubborn shadow of threat has gone.

He's safe now.

At least, his heart is safe.

He glances once more at the approaching flagship, all business now as his soldier instincts kick in. He juts his chin at the atlas. "And what do you plan to do with that?"

I look down at it in my hand, roll that scuffed plastic between the pads of my fingertips. I can't stop a mischievous grin—a grin very much like a fisherman I know—spread across my face.

"We'll take it to Arie," I announce, and look up into my love's waiting gaze, letting the wind blow strands of quicksilver hair out of my eyes. "Let her hunt down and destroy the Grandmaker before the Sons of Volok find him."

## DON'T MISS ANY OF THIS EPIC SERIES FROM D.V. SULLIVAN

## WWW.DVSULLIVAN.COM

# ABOUT THE AUTHOR

D.V. Sullivan has been a deckhand in the Mediterranean, a bartender in New York and an English teacher in China. Now that he's no longer hosing salt off yachts during high-wind gales, he writes from his lair in the Pacific Northwest.

DVSullivan.com
Facebook.com/AuthorDVSullivan
TikTok @dvsullivanauthor
Instagram @dvsullivanauthor
X/Twitter @bydvsullivan